LOST MOON

Book Two in a Post Magic World

LOST
MOON

Book Two in a Post Magic World

Ellis Logan

An Earth Lodge® Publication
Wallingford, Vermont

Published in the U.S.A. by Earth Lodge®
Cover Design by Maya Cointreau

ISBN 978-1-944396-90-9

An autumn night - don't think your life didn't matter.

- Matsuo Bashō

CHAPTER 1

*moons gather as one
half the city celebrates -
the remainder prays*

The silk of my dress was at it again. A shiver rose up my neck at the slight caress, a strange sensation of coolness and touch that kept occurring every time a breeze moved through the room, playing across the smooth green and white sheath.

My skin was jumpy, at odds with my mood. I twitched my shoulders in an effort to shake off the feeling even while I laughed at something outrageous Viv had said.

My cousin had spent our childhood walking a fine line and tonight was no different. The three moons of Renga had aligned two hours earlier and the Arch-mage of Chalinex was celebrating the semi-annual event with a massive gala. Everyone was invited to the Circle's headquarters, even non-magical regs – well, the rich and powerful ones, at any rate. Twins, Vivien and Ava were apprenticed to Arch-mage Spiren so I'd managed to score an invite, despite my humble origins as a post runner.

Not that I'd wanted to come. Power parties were not my scene. Family was important, though, whether forged by blood or water; when someone asked me to be there for them, I came.

Even when said event was crawling with threats and innuendo.

The rich regs in attendance had donned masks of tolerance to hide their fear and disdain of all chimeras, particularly the magically-empowered ones. The Enso, our self-regulating council, seemed happy to hob-nob with them and feign obeisance – though everyone knew that today the powers of almost every ket in the room had been heightened by the moons' convergence. Zyzygy may have been a day of celebration but the police would be heavily armed this night, just in case.

In case the sub-human chimeras made a grab for power; in case the genetically modified citizens of the city decided to speak out against the inequality they suffered. In case the Nekokai, the cat demons, decided to cause trouble.

As if that had ever happened.

As if we hadn't welcomed the regs open-armed when the came to our lands. We'd never given them any cause to fear us more than themselves, never committed as many violent crimes as they.

It mattered not. We were different, so people feared us. Not enough to shun our strange, tech-forsaken planet, more's the pity.

"Nikta, drink?"

Jericha's face was inches from mine, grinning.

"What?"

"You're a million parsecs away," my plus-one scolded. "I'm going to get some fresh drinks, you want a refill?"

I stared down at my sweet plum wine. Too sweet for a night like this. "No, some iced sake, please. The nigori from Novokyoto." I'd seen the potent pink delicacy parading by on a tray earlier in the night.

"Anything for my date," she winked and flounced away.

Viv watched my best friend's blonde head disappear into the crowd, reached out, and grabbed two pieces of sushi from a passing server. The waiter wasn't human, not even ket or another chimeric wonder. There was nothing genetic in the oversized automaton to modify. A scorpion-styled bot: born of steam, now fueled by magic. One burning coal could power the machine for two days, giving it life and motion. Its will hinged on something finer – the directive of the witch who had programmed it. In this case, the cool-headed, long-haired Ava. Where others might have seen the spiders and scorpions she created as creepy, my cousin saw a legacy of function and order. Grandmother spider, the creatress and story-weaver. Scorpion, the good mother who would only attack in defense.

I had to admit, their arching tales made ideal supports for the trays they carried while portraying the Enso's power. Ava's message tonight was clear, if unspoken: "*Do not bite the hand that feeds you.*"

Our ancestors had settled this world, allowed themselves to be genetically modified with panther DNA to increase their chances of survival in the chaline mines. The mods, the strange environment, something here had triggered magic in our souls. Unfortunately, as people had begun immigrating here from other planets, they hadn't all seen our evolution as wondrous or a blessing from the gods. They feared our alterations and powers despite the pains we took to do no harm, to blend in, to minimize our differences.

Some called us demons. Others, abominations. Here, tonight, I thought maybe Ava had the right idea. Since we were feared no matter what we did, perhaps openly claiming our uniqueness was a better tactic.

Handing me the delicately wrapped hand-roll of raw fish and young vegetables, Viv's coal-black eyes sparkled with mischief. "Speaking of dates, any word from that big bear you were seeing?"

"Kuma? No, nothing." I frowned, imagining the foreign poet traveling alone through the wilds for the hundredth time since I'd bid him goodbye. "I don't know where he headed after leaving the city last month. He could be anywhere."

Not dead, anywhere but in the ground or wounded, I hoped. The thought had become a mantra this week, worry creeping in unwanted and uninvited.

"Kuma's strong," I said brightly. "Wherever he is, I'm sure he's fine."

"Right," Viv agreed, though she eyed me thoughtfully. "He's a poet like you, isn't he? He's probably found some gorgeous mountaintop where he can write his next magnum opus."

"He's a professor, on sabbatical."

"Right, right. And you didn't want to ask him to stay a little longer, see what he could teach you?" she needled me.

"You know very well that I told him to go," I said, my sweet wine turning sour in my mouth.

"I do," she agreed quietly. "I'm still not sure why, though."

I hissed under my breath, starting to feel ornery. Viv was fire and she had a special talent for making emotions burn. But this wasn't the time or place. I closed my eyes, breathed out slowly, and watched the air around her fill with a cold mist, a fleeting cloak of white to match her pale spiked hair. The release yielded instant benefits, like turning a pressure valve on a steamer.

Better.

A few of the suits nearby muttered uneasily, moved further away.

"Careful, cousin, you're disturbing the eggs," Viv whispered, amused, using our childhood name for the regs who feared us. *So fragile, worse than chickens,* she'd once said. I could tell from her current tone she wouldn't much mind ruffling some feathers herself.

With Ava not around to cool her sister's temper, I realized I needed to get my own under control. Not all regs were bad, I reminded myself. I had plenty of non-gmo friends back in my hometown, Puraimura. Prime City had been settled first, it was the epicenter for colonization and terraforming on Renga, and it still boasted more kets than anywhere else. Chalinex, of all the cities on Renga, was its most shiny, modern cousin. More cultured, many said, citing the recent influxes of moneyed business people from distant planets. With the money and love of fine things, of course, they'd also brought corruption and greed.

I had avoided Chalinex for most of my life, despite the fact that my brother had moved here several years earlier. I'd missed him terribly, though, since he rarely responded to my letters. Finally, I'd had a chance to travel here for work last month when a fellow runner had needed some time off. By the time the month was out, I'd agreed to take on the entire zone as part of my new work assignment. Well, agreed might have been generous, as far as terms went. The lead detective at my brother's precinct hadn't exactly been in a negotiating kind of mood when he'd demanded my help on a case, something I'd been in a unique position to provide. As a special courier for the Peoples Galactic Postal Service, I could get in all sorts of places most people couldn't. The fact that I was a magically-endowed ket had only made my cooperation all the more attractive to the cops. I'd resisted but, in the end, yielded. The benefits – getting to see family more often, doing something to help those in need – had outweighed the negatives.

Or so I'd thought. Now, being bugged by my bratty cousin while wearing an uncomfortable new dress, I wasn't sure.

Viv laughed, almost as if she could read my thoughts. Exactly as if.

I swatted at her. "Stay out of my mind, cousin."

"Sorry, habit. Spiren's been making us practice our telepathy skills, though I can't say I've been having much success. Ava's still the only one I can easily read."

"I remember. Though you did always seem to know where I hid my candy," I reminded her. Ten years my elder, Viv and Ava had babysat Jonah and me for years. I had idolized them. And then they'd left Prime City. Left us.

She giggled, a sound that made my heart glow. "True. I could always read you when you were upset or excited. Anyone in the family, for that matter. But non-relatives? I have a much harder time. Ava's getting better at it, though."

"Maybe she's just better at listening."

"Probably. I'm not sure I want to hear anyone else's thoughts, anyways. Hearing my twin, it's more than enough, you know what I mean?"

"I do. I can't imagine having to hear Jonah's thoughts all the time. Though maybe if I did, we never would have grown so far apart. You and Ava are so close. I envy that."

"We have our ups and downs, just like you," she said. Never one to stay down for long, she wrapped me in a warm hug and then stood back, grinning. "Now, how about I get this party boosted? I think it's time to liven things up. Hang tight, I'll be back in five."

She hurried away and I sighed. I didn't want lively, I wanted the wilds. I'd only been in the city for four hours and already I felt dirty, polluted like the streets outside. I scanned the crowd for Jericha, found her flirting at the bar with a pretty, heavily pierced barmaid. Two glasses sat at her elbow, one a tantalizing shade of clouded pink. My rice wine. Apparently, my thirst scored lower than a possible new love interest. I didn't mind – I knew she'd been lonely since breaking up with her addict boyfriend a few weeks earlier – but this city air was making my throat itch. I started to cut through the crowd, planning to quietly grab my drink without interrupting anything.

I made it ten feet before my plans were foiled.

"Kitten! I should have known I'd meet you here." The voice was friendly, but I heard the sneer behind it.

I turned to face the long-haired man who'd dared caress my elbow. Mentally, I made a note to take a long, hot bath later. With soap. Lots and lots of soap.

"Mr. Lyell," I said, the name tasting sour in my mouth. "What a pleasure. I never did get to thank you for that wonderful introduction you gave me to your boss last month."

"My boss? Oh no, surely you misread the situation. He was merely an acquaintance. As you can see, I am here tonight, so I can't possibly have been involved in that debacle."

"Indeed," I drawled, taking in the fine cut of Axel Lyell's suit, the stunning red-head on his arm. One month earlier, Lyell had told a drug kingpin I was working with the cops. The result had not been pleasant. "I suppose I should thank you. If not for your introduction, I would never have discovered the source of the feed, nor been able to save a dear friend. You did me a great favor," I said, smiling slightly and bowing my head. "The Enso does not forget."

Lyell winced at the double meaning in my words and I noted the woman's painted talons digging into his arm as her grip tightened. Afraid? Or displeased to hear about his nefarious connections? I'd probably just ruined his chances to get lucky at the end of the evening. Amused by the possibility, deciding perhaps we were even, I bowed again.

"Nikta Kozan." I introduced myself to the woman. "I hope you are enjoying tonight's event."

"Yes," she purred in a husky voice. "It has been a most enlightening evening." She stuck out her hand, delicately gripping my own. "Annalee Brouillard, pleasure to meet you. So, you were part of the team that saved our city from that horrible drug?" she asked, referring to the feed, a mind-bending hallucinogen. "I must commend you."

"I played a small part, yes. But if you're looking for someone to thank, might I suggest a donation towards the rebuilding of Precinct 8?" I said, naming the station that had been bombed five weeks earlier. My brother's station. An officer had died that day, shredded along with several inner walls. Then, I remembered the city's poorest neighborhood. "Better yet, any organization working in the Mudlands would be great. There is such need there."

"Truly, there is." She smiled warmly. "You'll be happy to know that I already give a lot of attention to the children there and am quite involved in some programs to lift the teens there out of poverty."

Axel snorted and we both glared at him. "Sorry," he said quickly, paling under his escort's gaze. "I think the work you do is great, you know that." Perhaps he'd actually met his match in this one. Personally, I'd found Axel disturbingly skeezy and sensed Annalee might be far too good for him, but to each their own.

Behind Annalee, I caught sight of my brother. I'd known the cousins had invited him, but I'd never expected him to come. Surprised, my eyes widened.

"Old flame?" Annalee asked, sounding genuinely curious. Her eyes lingered over my brother's fine form, broad shoulders training with Cedar Secondary's swim team.

"No, thank Tara, no! A relative. He just made Detective, actually," I smirked at Axel. "Want to meet him?"

He stammered and I laughed. "Don't worry. We're all off-duty tonight. If you'll excuse me…" I left the unlikely pair and stalked off to greet my twin.

CHAPTER 2

pleasant smiles hide cold winds
damp matches that never light

"Ohalo, little brother," I called, waving to Jonah. Before he could stop me, I put my hand to his neck and pulled him in, touching my forehead to his in silent greeting. He might wish he'd never been born into our family, but he would always be a part of me. I felt his neck muscles tense under my grip even as he sighed and released him.

"Was that really necessary?" he whined, rubbing his face.

I ignored his words and spoke my own. "Fancy seeing you here, among the magicals. Or are you here as a representative of the CCPD?"

"I'm just here, okay? Can we leave it at that?"

"Sure, whatever you want," I said, grinning at him.

"Good." The relief was evident in his voice. "Actually, I came because I knew you'd be here."

"Hey, cuz!" Viv had bounced up, throwing an arm around each of us and drawing us in. "Did you bring a date? Because I told Ava to send you a plus one. I mean, I know it's hard, being, well, you, but I figured there must be someone who-"

She was interrupted by a loud cough. A small woman – fair, buxom, and most definitely not ket – stood before us unsmiling. "There is." She thrust out a hand, which Viv accepted after an awkward heartbeat. "Sargent Joyce Finelli."

"Ah. Hello." Viv blasted a 100-gigawatt smile, a smile so bright even my-stick-in-the-mud brother reciprocated. Sargent Finelli? Not so much. "Wonderful to meet you. Been dating long? You must tell us everything. Jonah hardly speaks to us."

"I can't imagine why not," Finelli said. Was that sarcasm?

I wasn't getting a warm vibe from the lady. But then, Jonah had always tried to be as un-ket as possible. Frankly, I was surprised he had even brought a friend from the precinct to meet us since I knew he'd been trying to keep his heritage a secret from his co-workers. Jonah could pass for human and he'd always liked it that way. He kept his magic under wraps and pretended he was as regular as he looked. I knew he found his heritage embarrassing, which begged the question, why was he here with a date?

Unless it was serious. Oh, Tara's toes. Could he really be thinking of marrying this humorless reg? I decided to put forth my best behavior, just in case.

"Ohalo, Joyce. I'm Nikta. Welcome to the Circle," I said, using the reg name for the Enso. "It's so nice to meet one of Jonah's friends from work. He's very happy there."

"He should be." She beamed with pride. "Has he told you that he made Detective last month?"

"Yes, he did," I said, smiling back at her. I would not diminish the accomplishment by pointing out that he had not earned the post entirely on his own, that I had been the one to demand his promotion in return for my continuance as contractor with the CCPD. Jonah didn't know I'd made it a condition of my contract and I planned to keep it that way. He was so stubborn, so contrary, he would probably abandon the post if he knew. I couldn't allow that, not when he actually deserved the promotion. He was a good cop. A shit brother, but a generally good person.

"We are very proud," I said instead.

Viv opened her mouth to speak and I whipped a tendril of ice cold air down her throat before she could blurt out something that would ruin the moment. She bit back a grin, understanding, and nodded. "Let me find Ava, she'll want to say hello. And you both must meet Spiren before the night is over, too." She stalked away, but I only had eyes for Joyce. Her expression had gone from general distaste to clear nervousness at the mention of the Arch-mage. Whatever her feelings for Jonah, she clearly held no good will for magic.

What had he told her? Did she even know Jonah had powers of his own? Suddenly, my own nerves were jangling. I had little tolerance for subterfuge.

"So, Nikta, any news from Prime?" Jonah saved me, trying to fill the silence. Usually, I was the one to make overtures between us – everything about tonight was different.

I cocked my head, considering. "Not really. Jericha's single again, though I don't think that's gonna last long." I gestured towards the bar with my chin and Jonah laughed. Jericha's lips were puckered and she was leaning forward to let the bartender apply a bright red gloss to them.

"Another cousin?" Joyce asked, arching one brow.

"An old friend," Jonah said, and I added, "Like family."

Joyce chewed her bottom lip and I realize she'd misunderstood.

"Jericha's my best friend. But don't worry," I said conspiratorially, "Jonah never dated her."

"Not that Jerrie didn't try," Jonah boasted and Joyce's mouth tightened. I thought about smacking Jonah in the forehead. What an idiot he was. Couldn't he see Joyce didn't want to know these kinds of things? Again, I wondered why he'd brought her here.

"So, Joyce, tell me about yourself. Did you grow up in Chalinex?"

"Mmm, yes, and what are your intentions towards our baby cousin?" Viv butted in before Joyce could answer me, rejoining our group with Ava and the Arch-mage on her arm.

Joyce's jaw dropped and suddenly she looked ten years younger. Small and afraid. Ava and Viv certainly made a stunning pair, both with ice-white hair and night-black eyes, dressed in similarly draped floor-length silvery gowns with deep plunging V's – though of course where Ava wore hers to expose her back, her long hair piled high upon her head in twisting braids, Viv's dress slashed down between her breasts. But it was at the Arch-mage the policewoman stared. I couldn't blame her. He was incredibly tall with the build of a willow, his long black hair queued down his back. His face boasted strong cheekbones and skin that defied what I knew was an advanced age. Only the deep crinkles beside each eye betrayed his years and, I assumed, a good humor.

"Leave her alone, Viv," Jonah said irritably, which seemed to snap Joyce out of her reverie. She looked at me, color rising in her cheeks as she realized she'd forgotten to answer me.

"Yes, I was born here. My parents immigrated from Sector 89-T."

"Why, that's halfway across the galaxy!" Ava exclaimed. "What brought them here? I'm Ava, by the way, Vivien's sister. I gather you met?"

"Yes, we met. Joyce Finelli. Nice to meet you," she said in a tone that gave lie to her words. "My parents were missionaries, they traveled all over before landing here."

"Couldn't resist our beautiful planet, eh? Juniper Spiren, pleasure."

Joyce shook the Arch-mage's hand, looking unhappy. "You could say that. They felt called here, said they could not forsake any planet so godless as Renga."

"Godless!" Ava exclaimed. "But we have many gods."

"And the festivals to prove it," Viv joked.

Joyce's lower lip jutted out in a pout. "Many gods, but no true reverence. Faith is not about festivals, it is about devotion to the one God."

"Ah. I see." Ava peered at Joyce thoughtfully. "Thankfully, Renga has always been a welcoming planet. Easy to terraform, easy to love. And we welcome all kinds and faiths. Is this not why we gather tonight in celebration, to celebrate the union of the moons themselves, our very own holy trinity?"

Joyce hissed, a ket-like sound if I ever heard one. Somehow, I knew she would not take kindly to the comparison. "There is nothing holy about moon worship."

"Easy ladies. Tonight we come together as a circle of all faiths. There are no sides, no ends, no beginnings. There is room for everyone here. Please," The Archmage urged and I could feel the tension leaving the group. Something about his voice... was this his magic? Was this how he had risen through the ranks to become one of the most powerful men in the city? If so, this was a gift I could stand to learn, my social graces often as lacking as Viv's. "Now, if you'll excuse me, I must continue making the rounds. Nikta, a pleasure seeing you again. Detective Kozan, Officer Finelli. Girls, if you'll join me? I have some people I'd like you to meet."

He gave us a slight bow and walked away, Ava and Viv flanking him. Joyce watched them go, then excused herself to find the bathroom. I whirled on Jonah.

"Why did you bring her here? Did you know how she felt? How can you date her?" The questions burst forth without planning.

Jonah's fists clenched. "People are staring," he ground out.

"Sorry," I said in a low tone. "Wouldn't want anyone to think you're a racist. Oh. Wait. Too late."

"That's not fair," he complained, his eyes flashing with an inner fire. Good, he was mad. So was I.

"You're right. You're just dating one. Does she even know you have magic?"

Jonah squirmed, the light in his eyes shuttering.

"Dammit, Jonah. What are you thinking? You can't hide your true nature, it's not healthy. You'll only wind up hurting yourself, or her. Besides, what if you get married, have babies – what do you think she's going to do if she has kittens? Kittens who can control the wind, make fire, change the flow of water? Do you think she'll still love you then?"

"She's not as bad as you think," he muttered.

"For my brother, she needs to be the moons and the stars and everything in between. Not just "not that bad." Sometimes, I just don't know where your head is at, I swear."

"She only found out I'm even part ket last month, you know, after the bombing. I think she's come around nicely in such a short time."

"Part ket?" I blinked, unable to credit what I'd just heard. "Jonah, you couldn't be more ket if you'd been one of the first settlers. Just because you don't have mama's ears or papa's eyes, doesn't change who or what you are."

"Shh," he shushed me. "She's coming. Please, Nikta, just give her a chance. She's giving you one."

"Giving me-" I broke off, too angry to speak. Which was for the best, because Joyce was indeed approaching.

"Hi, guys. You didn't have to wait for me out here," she said shyly to Jonah, blushing. Then she looked at me. "I'm sorry about all that in there. Sometimes, my past gets the better of me. My parents, they raised me to fear magic. The Enso. All of this." She gestured back towards the party. "I was terrified to come here, to meet you, frankly. But I've been trying to see things your way, your brother's way."

"That's good," I managed, giving her a wan smile, not wanting to tell her that Jonah's way had not been my way for many years. "All I want is for Jonah to be happy."

"Me, too," she said.

"Which I am," he said, taking her hand in his, giving it a squeeze. "Very."

"Good," I repeated, trying hard to mean it. "Listen, I have a bunch of letters to deliver early tomorrow and I don't think that sushi is sitting well with me. I'm going to retire to my room and get some rest. Can you tell Jericha I've released her from duty as my date?"

"Of course," he said, cocking his head towards the ballroom. "Though I don't think she'll miss you."

"No, she'll do fine without me. Like you," I said and kissed his cheek. "Goodnight, little brother. It was good to meet you, Joyce." I inclined my head deeply, not caring to see whether she returned my bow.

I left quickly, navigating the hallways of the Enso through blurred vision, tears threatening to fall. But I would not cry. Not tonight. Not for my brother's newest folly.

I retreated into my room, sealing the door with ice that would melt only by my command, sealing out the noise of the party, of disappointing siblings and meddling cousins. I collapsed onto the soft feather bed covering my tatami mat and clenched my hands into fists, extinguishing the lights in the room. Above me, clear through the glass, stars glimmered companionably; swirling clouds of nebulous gasses twinkling and shifting; three moons overlaid just above the horizon in near concentric circles of blue, white, pink.

CHAPTER 3

dawn comes, a new day
the rooster crows false greeting
ere it flies away

I didn't sleep. Too many thoughts. Too much anger touched with an overabundance of sadness, loneliness. I'd written a haiku for each emotion as it tore through my head but the verses had offered no relief. Frustrated, I'd burned them all with a flick of my hand before giving up on creativity, on sleep, and sitting seiza before the one-way glass. Buttocks resting comfortably on heels, I bowed my head in prayer and entered into a long string of prayer. I chose the ancient metta bhavana mantras: compassion for my loved ones, compassion for my enemies, compassion for myself.

This last one was a real sticking point.

How often had I blamed myself for Jonah's problems? How many times had I been the one to reach out, only to be rebuffed? Twins were supposed to be close, two pieces of a whole like Viv and Ava, but no amount of gold seemed able to reforge the broken bowl that was our relationship. Sometime in the early morning hours, long after Hokku had set, hours before it would rise again, I reached a point of stillness. A quiet within the soul. And in the peace I saw my grandfather's face, remembered his last words. Jonah had run to Chalinex after our mother had died, left Jiji even as he had begun to ail, and the sting of his abandonment had prompted me to tuck my heart deep behind thick skin no one else could prick.

"Do not forget the love you had for your brother when you were children. When I am gone, you both will need each other to heal. You will have to be mother, father, grandfather to each other. Neither of you can be who you were meant to be if you remain apart."

Oh, how I had tried. Tried to ignore the pain in my heart, the missing of Jonah. The wilds had been my happy place, paths I'd long traveled with Jiji in training to be a post runner. So, I'd thrown myself into the forest. Found joy in the solitude and kept love at bay.

One sick courier and a chance to visit my brother in Chalinex City had ripped my illusions apart. One piece of mail that never should have been delivered, and everything had changed. Someone working with Lyell's boss had tried to send my brother's precinct a message, tried to kill the lead detective investigating the kingpin by sending a bomb through the mail. I had unwittingly hand-delivered the package, forever changing my life path. I'd been asked to work for the detective who'd lived through the blast, conscripted to work undercover on the case or face prosecution. Unfair, but typical for the CCPD. I'd agreed, more out of a desire to look out for Jonah than anything else. Worked the case, then signed on for more. In just a few short weeks I'd become an associate of the Enso, under the protection of the CCPD, all while continuing to run some of the most sensitive mail for the PGPS.

I'd gone from having few connections to navigating a sticky web of power and magic.

Was this who I was meant to be?

Truly, I didn't know. All I could do was give myself over to Tara and pray for her blessings. Scratch that – I was pretty sure I'd need the blessings of all my ancestors, all my guides and totems, before I found my way true.

"Om tare tuttare ture soha."

I gave myself over to Tara, She Who Saves, the enlightened one of liberation and compassion, and rose only when my stomach complained for breakfast.

Outside my door, nothing had changed since the evening before, but I felt lighter. Ready to face a new day. Something had shifted inside me, bringing me back to center. I pulled on my travel clothes: rugged leggings and a net shirt over clean underthings, topped with an ankle-length sweater vest knit from resilient silken fibers. Dark blue patterned with muted leaves, the vest had been a gift from my mother designed to cloak my presence in the wilds. I never left Prime without it.

I faced the door, placed a hand on the wood and inhaled deeply, drawing the power I'd left there back into me. Waste not, want not. The shield dropped.

In the hallway, all was quiet. No, not all. I cocked an ear, listening to the slight approaching scuttle. Not human, I decided. Moments later, a small spider automaton crept into view and I placed a finger to my lips.

"Shh, don't wake your masters," I warned the Enso's butler. "All I need is a snack."

The spider dipped twice in acknowledgment then turned and hastened down the hall, stopping at a corner to beckon me to follow it towards the kitchens.

The Enso had its own cook, a woman who came in for several hours each morning to prepare dishes, but it was far too early in the day to run into her. Even if it had been later, I imagined the woman had earned a day off after all the work she'd done overseeing the catering for the gala. She'd created a feast fit for the modern lords and ladies of the city, surely they couldn't have devoured it all, I thought. I gazed around the impressive kitchen, barely paying mind to the heavy copper pots hanging from a wide cedar bough above the central island. If I could just find where she'd hidden the appetizers, I wouldn't have to fire up the massive stove or trespass into the cook's costly collection of solid-core calressium knives. My eyes landed on a handsomely carved door at the other end of the room, the tell-tale signs of ice magic frosting its edges.

"Hello, cold storage," I murmured appreciatively.

Five minutes later, I was sitting down at the island with to a satisfying meal of bite-sized smoked kale and trout sausages, dipping each one into a bowl of sweet apricot ketchup as I ate. After cleaning up, I spread my scheduled deliveries out on the table to plot the day's route. I was pleased to note one thin envelope with a familiar destination. Deciding to save the best for last rather than focus on expediency, I mapped my route accordingly.

Three small packages to the fancy estates on the east side where the rich had been savvy in their land grabs, laying claim to the part of the city hit first by prevailing winds and rains. The waters came down daily, cleansing their streets of filth and depositing them downwind. Far on the other side of the city to the southwest, the grime and corruption would come to pool in the Mudlands – the impoverished slums of Chalinex City.

A shoe-sized box and an oversized letter tube destined for the business district. Jericha's flat bordered the area, so I was already familiar with some of the merchants and noodle shops.

Last, the Mudlands where I had one thin letter headed for Zenta Road. The slimness of the tube nagged at me; I hoped it held good news.

Running helped alleviate some of the strain. Jiji had started Jonah and me on the trail as children, strengthening our limbs so that if we needed to we could run for days on end. My feet were tough, thickly padded from the years of training, cushioning my stride while my thin canvas boots protected me from the dirt and hazards of the streets. Running was like breathing, the best of meditations, and I chided myself for not having gone on a run the night before. If I had, I probably would have sunk into sleep with ease. Oh well. Tonight I'd be clear of the city, free in the wilds, and I was sure I would find my peace there.

Soon, I assured myself and ran on. Over the drawbridges of the Amaitomi river, through the wealthiest neighborhoods in the city. The river wrapped around the north and east quadrants of Chalinex and yielded a sweet, mineral-heavy water that was believed to lend health benefits to the locals. Centuries earlier, it had been used to transport chaline from local mines to processing centers. Now, it served as a natural barrier between the haves and the have nots. Rich lords and ladies, second sons and neglected daughters who had made their way to our small planet to become richer, enticed by the lack of infrastructure, the dearth of technology. To them, Renga presented an easy place to make their mark. Of course, they never settled in my hometown of Puraimura, a backwater city even for Renga. Too many locals and not enough culture, they complained, code for too-many kets and our simple ways. In Prime, we observed the festivals as a community: life was less shiny, more real. In Chalinex everything glittered, but the streets were dirty, the cops on the take. Kets represented the minority, many of them relegated to living in the ghettos of the Mudlands to the south.

I made my deliveries as quickly as I could, overwhelmed by the opulent wealth of the North Bank; wealth I knew often came at the expense of regular working class people like me. Leaving the ritzy neighborhood behind, I jogged through the middle-class neighborhoods, places that reminded me more of home. Families in charming duplexes with small yards, trying to get by, live a good life.

Eventually, open-air plazas gave way to corner marketplaces where I made two more deliveries, picked up some dried fruits and jerky for the trail. And ran on. Neatly manicured parks morphed into ramshackle lots with broken swings, apartments became low-income tenements, and finally, the crowded slums of the Mudlands.

Still, I pressed on until I found myself among the worst Chalinex had to offer, picking my way through the broken glass, burning piles of trash, and busted bicycles of Zenta Road. I counted the blocks, each side of the road dominated with a sprawling project. Two. Six. Eight. Fourteen. I didn't slow, dashing up the front stoop between several men who may or may not have been sleeping. Through the gaping aluminum doorframes, the glass in them long cracked and knocked away. Up the stairs. No point trying the elevator – in a place like this, it was safer not to get boxed in, even if I was lucky enough to find it working. Holding my breath, trying not to breath in the stench of refuse, vomit, and worse. The relief when I emerged on the eighth floor, let the door to the stairwell slam behind me.

Here, the air was stale but palatable, filled with cooking spices, incense, perfumes. And still, I jogged down the endless hall, almost the length of the building, until I came to apartment 8JJ. For the first time in miles, I smiled. And knocked.

The elderly Pablo Gunjabmi opened the door. "Ohalo, sir. I have another special delivery for you."

Pablo smiled at me and urged me to come in, quickly closing the door behind us. This, I'd learned, was not only hospitable but wise. The Gunjabmis' grandson had a habit of sending the money every couple weeks, a dangerous gift to be receiving here in the Mudlands where my day's wages could keep a family in food for a month.

"Omma, look, our friend Nicola has come again," he called happily.

His wife bustled forward and laughed, taking my hand. "It's Nikta, Pablo, you silly old man. He'd forget the hat on his head if it weren't for me," she confided in a stage whisper.

"No worries, it's my job to remember you, not the other way around," I grinned. I'd only met them once before, but I loved this family. They reminded me of my own, my home before everyone I loved had died or left Puraimura. Several kids watched us over the back of a sofa and a toddler waddled over, grasping her Omma's skirt in one hand while she sucked loudly on the other thumb and stared up at me with large, curious eyes. Obliging, I dug into my pack and pulled out my last package: the small, thin scroll with the Gunjabmi's direction carefully written on its tube enclosure. "Here, this is for you."

Pablo took it, carefully weighing it in one wrinkled palm. "It's been so long since his last letter. And it doesn't weigh much. What can it say?" His voice betrayed a shiver of worry as his watery eyes connected with Omma's.

"Go on, don't be a ninny. Open it," she urged. She smiled, but I saw Pablo's concern reflected in her gaze.

He unsealed the tube and unrolled the scroll within. "It's short," he said. "No money this time, obviously."

"Has he saved up enough?" one of the children called. "Is he sending for us already?"

I knew their eldest brother had been working to save for a houseboat for the whole family on the island planet of Perseus and I felt a twinge of excitement. Would the Gunjabmi's be getting out of this hellhole sooner than expected?

"It says...Hello, Omma, Buelo. I know you must be worried because it has been so long since I sent any funds. Unfortunately, I will be unable to send anything for the coming year or more. We are heading into Deep Space on an extended mission and will have no access to Galactic agencies. I am sorry. Henry."

Pablo frowned, looked at the back of the letter as if it might hold more answers. It was blank.

The mood in the room plummeted and for a moment no one seemed to know what to say. Omma was the first to break the silence.

"That's it? But no, that can't be right! Something is wrong, Pablo, I just know it. I told you last week, we must go to the authorities, put out a search-"

"Please, Omma, we've been over this. Henry is a grown man now. We have to trust that he knows what he is doing. You mustn't worry, you're upsetting the children again. We'll find a way to get by. We always have."

"I'm not worried about that, you fool!" she snapped, then lowered her voice. "I'm worried about Henry! We've lost enough of our family, I won't lose Henry, too, not if there is something that can be done. He's gotten into trouble, I know it. Look here! He signed it 'Henry.' Not Rooster. Henry. It's not right." She shoved the letter back in Pablo's face and then burst into tears.

I rubbed her shoulder, wanting to console her. "Children, go to your room," Pablo said in a low voice. Quickly, they filed out, the eldest, a thin girl of but nine or ten stooping to cradle the now-crying toddler in her arms.

"I feel terrible," I said. "Is there anything I can do?"

"No, please. This is not your concern. My wife likes to worry. I am sure our grandson is fine, making lots of money somewhere. He'll be back soon, you'll see."

Omma shook her head, wiping her eyes to peer up at me with sodden lashes. "He won't, I can feel it. This is just how I felt when Elaina went missing, before they found her body. First, his mother, and now Henry! Oh, I can't bear it."

"Please, Omma, you're getting worked up over nothing," Pablo pleaded with her, looking apologetically at me.

"Look," I said. "Why don't you give me the letter? Write down whatever information you have about the ship he's on, when he started working there, all of that. I have connections at the CCPD. I'm sure they'd be happy to look into it." Actually, I was pretty sure Jonah would have zero interest in helping anyone from the Mudlands – not my precinct, he'd probably say – but I thought maybe if I played the sister card, just maybe, he might do it.

"Would you do that, truly? But you hardly know us?" Omma said wonderingly.

"You remind me of some people I lost, too. Please, let me do this for you. My ancestors will smile on us both."

"If you really don't mind," Pablo said, hugging his wife to him with one arm. "You would put our minds at ease. Even I must admit, it is strange for Henry to sign his name as he did. He has long used the nickname

'Rooster.' Claimed he was lucky, not destined for the pot like some Mudlands hen."

"And he used to write us every few days, send money every two weeks, even though I told him we did not need so much. But this is the first we've heard from him in over a month."

"Since the last time he sent you money?" I asked, remembering when we'd met. Pablo walked to the small kitchen table, wrote something down.

"Yes, since then. It's not normal," she insisted, stubborn with courage now, her chin jutting out. "He's in trouble."

"Here," Pablo said, handing me a piece of rough, poorly-made paper. It struck me that even the smallest of things were lacking here in Mudlands, hard to come by, low of quality. No wonder Henry had insisted on sending them as much as he could. Which made me wonder, was Omma right? Would Henry really have left them with so little warning, without sending at least some small token to tide them over while he was out of range? "This is everything I know about where Henry went. It's not much. The name of his ship, the day he left for Hokku, the captain of the ship. I hope you can find something out, anything that will put our minds at ease."

"I will do my best, I swear, and I will come back as soon as I know something. It may be a week or more, so try not to worry if I do not come right back. I have to head back to Puraimura to complete my route before I return here. But I'll go to the station today, give them this information, and hopefully we will know something soon. Do you have a telephone here you can be reached at?"

Pablo shook his head. "The building lost service two years ago, and the Tel-Com refuses to come back and repair it. They say there's no point, not when the gangs are constantly stealing the wires for scrap money. There's one phone four blocks away at the market, no one dares steal their cables, since they supply all the food in the neighborhood. I'll give you their number. They know how to find me."

"Okay," I said, my stomach wrenching. How could the city let this happen? So many things needed to be fixed here, it was hard to know where to start. At least I could help them with Henry.

I hoped.

CHAPTER 4

*water streaming, questions drop
to the rhythm of a song*

I left the Mudlands moving fast without really seeing. If I'd been in Henry's position, I would never abandon my family. I would have worked for their welfare as long as I could, just as he had been doing. *As long as I could.* Was something keeping him from doing just that, as the Gunjabmi's feared? He had to know what his letters meant to the family, how hard they struggled. It seemed unlikely he would take an extended mission, no matter the payout. Was he being forced to do something he didn't want, or was it something else – a girl, maybe? Did he perhaps suffer from the same brand of thoughtlessness that Jonah had always exhibited, putting his own desires above family? I wasn't sure which would be worse. The former could mean Henry was in real trouble; the latter, the Gunjabmi's had truly been set aside, possibly condemned to a sinking sort of life in the Mudlands.

I'd stayed a few extra minutes with the family, praising the little ones' drawings, though they'd been a little hard to see clearly in the dimly lit apartment. Only one light had been burning in the apartment, a rosy grow-lamp above a prolific wall-garden filled with herbs and fresh greens. The rest of their living space had been illuminated only by the large windows along an outer wall.

Last in a long string of planets, Renga was so far from the closest sun that the star appeared only as a distant glimmer in the sky. Luckily, there was more than enough ambient light and warming galactic radiation to keep us warm, our sky an ever-shifting tapestry of nebulae lighting our moons from all angles and creating a never-ending twilight scenario. Most buildings were built with ample windows and no curtains. Renga had been a hot destination for health nuts trying to escape the effects of technology, especially since someone had published a study in the early years about how the cosmic cocktails of vitamins pelting the planet could benefit a body, assuming you were able to soak them up for at least eighty percent of your day to keep away any deficiencies. Kets could get by with about half that amount since we'd been engineered for the mines, but it didn't do good things for our mood.

I'd almost asked Omma to turn on a light but then thought better of it. No matter how they denied it, they must really have been hurting for money if they were skimping on electricity. We didn't have much here in the way of technology, but working plumbing, electric lights, and basic telephone service were basic amenities. While the rest of the universe played on holo-decks and spent half their lives inside computers, many of us here still owned gramophones and attended acoustic concerts. But no one lived in the dark.

I frowned. A pelting rain had started up to match my mood, the kind of warm downpour where each drop seemed to hold an ounce of water. It didn't matter. I was used to getting wet – it rained frequently here on Renga, even more often around Zyzygy. This was probably the first of several days of heavy rains. Pedestrians began to clear the streets, searching for shelter, and I no longer had to carefully plot my path among them. Grateful, I tilted my face towards the darkened sky and picked up my pace, enjoying the feel of the water streaming down my arms. I gave myself over to the run, enjoying it so much that I almost didn't stop when I came to Precinct 8.

Steeling myself, I slowed my pace and walked into my brother's domain. The desk-sergeant was unfamiliar, a young woman who smiled in greeting. New, obviously, as yet unjaded by the grind. I smiled back and ran a hand through my hair, pushing the short, dripping strands back between my ket ears where I knew they would mimic a hyena's spiked mane.

"Hi there, how can I help you?" the cop asked cheerfully, barely sparing my ears a second glance. I couldn't help noting her seeming lack of bias, rare here in the department.

"Yes, thank you. My name is Nikta Kozan, I have urgent business with Detective Pearce."

"Sure, let me see... Do you have an appointment?" She traced her finger down the desk log, biting her lip in concentration.

"No, I don't. But I have this." I flipped up the lapel of my sweater, flashed the small pin that Lyric had put there over a month before. I could have also used my PGPS-issued calressium bangle to get access, no one ever denied a special carrier entry, but I knew that a CCPD token would hold more influence in this building. Lyric called it my "Get out of jail free" card; I called it extortion, the dues I had exchanged to see my brother more often.

The young woman's mouth formed an "O" in surprise upon seeing the badge marking me as someone under the police department's protection.

"Oh, I see! So sorry to keep you waiting, ma'am! Please, go right in. You know where his office is? If anyone bothers you, you just tell them Bex Montana sent you in."

I wasn't sure whether to be pleased by her cooperation, a far cry from the surly bigotry of the usual desk-jockeys here, or annoyed. She'd called me ma'am. How old did she think I was? Surely only a few years her senior, hardly enough to be called a ma'am. I decided to chalk it up for respect for my position as someone of possible importance, rather than any premature aging I might be experiencing. Still, it wouldn't hurt steep a few qualitchka leaves in oil the next time I got home. After a few weeks infusing in a cool cabinet, the resulting oil would be perfect as a base for a regenerative beauty balm. Maybe I'd add some essence from the skin of one of my Meyer lemons, too, to jumpstart the cellular healing.

"Ma'am?" Bex said. "You can go in now."

"Oh, right! Sorry, I was just figuring something out," I confided, flushing.

"For a case?" she gushed. "That must be so exciting. You're so lucky, working with Detective Pearce. I joined this precinct specifically because I hope to work under him someday."

"You want to be a detective?" I asked, surprised. It was just about the last thing I'd ever considered for a profession. I had never wanted anything other than to follow in my family's footsteps and be a post runner like my ojisan before me. My family had been navigating the wilds practically since Renga had been settled, and the pack I carried now was a legacy of that. Jiji claimed it had made its way here from First Earth itself, a true relic of the past, though I'd secretly always doubted the leather could possibly be that old. Still, I cared for it regularly, carefully cleaning and oiling the leather after every run, exactly the way my grandfather had taught me.

"It's why I joined." She nodded. "My father was a cop, though he quit when I was just a kid. Drinking," she whispered. "Anyway, there was a horrible murder at my school just before graduation. Everyone guessed what had happened, but no one could prove it. Then, Pearce took up the case," she sighed dreamily.

"Let me guess," I dead-panned. "He nailed the killer?"

"Yeah, he did. I knew then I wanted to do what he did. You know, save the day? Make people feel safe?"

"That's great," I said, edging towards the door. "Well, I think you made the right choice. I definitely feel better knowing someone like you is on the force." *Someone who doesn't mind talking to ket*, I thought. *Someone who cares about the lives they saved – about living.*

"Ohalo, Kozan-san," she said, bowing.

"Ohalo, Officer Montana." I smiled and slid inside the inner sanctum of the precinct. Cops bustled to and fro, filing paperwork, taking statements. No one paid me any mind. Lyric wasn't in his office and I stood there a moment, marveling at the changes. The original walls had been repaired since they'd been blown out, erasing the reminder of Duffy Merit's final moments.

It had been a mess. A package I'd carried and delivered had contained a bomb, and Pearce's assistant had been opening the mail when it literally blew up in his face. Talk about putting your life on the line for a job. I'd been pulled in for questioning, coerced into helping Pearce do some undercover work, and helped crack the case. The drug dealer peddling magical oblivion had disappeared and the production line had been shut down. Pearce had been so impressed with my work (and my connections at the Enso) that he'd asked me to stay on as a part-time consultant for his department. I'd agreed, but only once he agreed to promote Jonah in return. Jonah would have been so mad to know his big sister had butted into his life. Again. He'd had a chip on his shoulder ever since he'd been disqualified from the Pan-Galactic Olympics just for being a chimera. Not that he hadn't known the rules going into his career as a swimmer – but still. He'd been mad at the world ever since. Mad at me, at everything ket.

Realizing I had no business standing in Pearce's office, I proceeded over to Jonah's desk. "Nikta!" Jonah barked in surprise, louder than he intended. "What are you doing here?"

For a moment I couldn't remember. Jonah. Lyric. Bex. My mind back-peddled and then I had it. "The Gunjabmis," I said, stalking forward and plonking my pack on the chair in front of his desk. "One of my regular stops. Their grandson sends them money regularly through special post, helps take care of his younger siblings. The parents are dead, so everyone is counting on him to help get them out of the Mudlands. And he's been doing a good job of it, too. Put a deposit down on a boat in Perseus and everything. But today he sent them this."

I tossed Henry's letter in front of him, watched him scan its contents with a furrowed brow. Watched the lines smooth out.

"Looks like he's done a runner." He leaned back, angled his head to one side and looked me. "What do

41

you want from me, Nikta? Do you need me to call in social services? Are the grandparents unsuitable guardians?"

"No, no, nothing like that. They're great. Amazing, actually. I mean, it's a bit tight for them without Henry sending money, but I think they can scrape by. The problem is, they think something's wrong. Henry could be in trouble."

"Then they need to go to their local precinct and file a missing person report."

"Why bother?" I retorted. "They live in the Mudlands, on Zenta Street. You know as well as I do that no one will help them. These are good people, Jonah. Trust me."

He eyed me warily, leaning back in his chair as if trying to put more distance between us. "I trust you, Tara save me." He sighed. "But this is out of my jurisdiction. I've barely just made detective, sister, I can't start calling in favors for a kid who's probably off getting laid."

"I don't think-"

Jonah cut off whatever defense I was about to play. "Tell the family to go to their local authorities. I can't get in the middle of this. I've got rules to follow here."

Heat rose through my body, the air around me shimmering slightly and I opened my mouth to speak. A cool hand clamped down on my arm, squeezing gently, and I almost jumped out of my seat, my teeth grinding together in surprise. A jolt of energy burst out of me without intention, blowing a stack of papers off Jonah's desk up into his lap.

"Easy, runner," a voice said with authority and just a hint of humor. "Let's save our family dramas for the home, please."

"Pearce," Jonah said, cheeks darkening. "I apologize for my sister here. I'm taking care of it, please don't worry."

"Taking care of it?" I derided. I twisted in my chair to look up Lyric, whose hand had moved to my shoulder. "He's not taking care of anything. I've got a family in trouble and he refuses to even look into it."

"Your family?" Lyric asked, surprised.

"No. PGPS clients. Good people," I said, glaring at Jonah pointedly.

"Guy was taking care of his family, sending home money every so often and now he's run off into Deep Space. They're concerned, but it sounds like a family matter, not a missing person," Jonah said defensively. "Besides, they're from the Mudlands. It's not our jurisdiction, as I told my sister."

"Hmm. Maybe not." He'd removed his hand from my shoulder and was twisting the gold wedding band on one finger absent-mindedly. "But the cops over there have more than their fair share of casework. Tell me more. Maybe I can do something – but I'm not making any promises."

"Anything you can do has got to be better than that joke of a precinct in the Mudlands. No offense."

"None taken. I've heard the stories, cases falling through the cracks, more criminals than cops to go around. So, what's this guy's story?"

"He's a kid, really. Not even twenty yet. He found shipwork on Hokku and has been running missions, sending back money every two weeks. He dotes on his little sisters and brothers, from everything I've heard. He wouldn't just bail on them."

"Not even if something better came along?"

I shook my head. "No. I don't think so. Look here, where he signed his name."

"So?"

"It's wrong. His grandparents say he always signs his letters home 'Rooster.' It's his lucky name, kind of a family joke. Something's not right here. Can you look into it, please?"

"Sure, it's been a slow week. I can make some inquiries. Come on, we'll fill out a report."

He led me to his office. I couldn't help turning around, sticking my tongue out at Jonah before I entered and my brother rolled his eyes with a smirk. Some things never changed. No matter how much we grew up or apart, part of us would always be five years old, pulling each others' hair.

I spent the next five minutes writing out everything I could think of, then watched Lyric fill out an official investigative request.

"Can you spell his last name again for me?" He asked. I spelled it out and watched him write every letter. He splayed his hands out on the paper, then folded his fingers together. "Anything else I can do for you today?" he asked, lifting one eyebrow, his pale green eyes more patient than usual.

"No, that's all. Thank you so much, Lyric, I really appreciate it."

"This family's really made an impression on you, huh?" He seemed amused and I bristled, though I couldn't have said why.

"I have a soft spot for family that looks out for each other. It's something...well, I miss it."

"You look out for your brother."

"Yes, but who does he look out for?" I asked before I could stop myself. I puffed out my cheeks, exhaling slowly. "Sorry. I shouldn't have-"

"It's okay. I won't say anything to him, if that's what worries you."

"It's just- It wasn't appropriate. You're his boss. It wasn't face-saving."

"Family is tough," he said cryptically. Something in his expression shuttered and he stood abruptly. "I'll look into your case. Now, if you'll excuse me, Miss Kozan? I have some other things that need my attention."

"Oh! Yes, of course. My apologies *Detective* Pearce. I'll be back within the week. Thank you, really." I ducked my head several times, grabbing my pack and backing out of the room. "Ohalo."

"Ohalo," he said quietly, then sat back down without sparing me another glance.

Well, I thought, hurrying back out onto the street, waving to Bex as I left. That had been weird. But it didn't matter, I thought, a smile catching fire between my cheeks. Pearce was on the case. And soon, devas willing, Henry would be found.

CHAPTER 5

empty nest, sad heart
drinks flow when blood's apart
Lo! false idols

I didn't waste any time leaving the city, grabbing letters destined for Puraimura and Hokku from the central Chalinex PGPS headquarters and escaping to the fresh air of the wilds.

Normally, this would have been all I needed to relax but I was restless, barely stopping to enjoy making camp each night or chat at the handful of drop-offs I made. I didn't want to think about Henry or Jonah, but whenever I tried to clear my head, it would fill instead with memories of Kuma.

Of the nights we'd spent in the forest, the places we'd made love, the laughs we'd shared and the promises I'd refused to make.

I'd allowed only one – that he'd keep in touch while he explored our world on his writer's walkabout.

I had yet to receive a single letter.

I hissed, kicking a stone ahead of me as I jogged and slid down a muddy hill into the valley of Prime. This was why I didn't like relationships. I had no time for false promises, and no yen for anything permanent. I was young, I was free, and I enjoyed my life. Well, most of it, anyway. Things were looking up with my brother, and if I had to sacrifice a bit of my safety in exchange for increased access to his station, I could live with that. I'd told Kuma I didn't want anything from him, so why was I so mad that he hadn't written?

He'd probably found some sweet young pioneer to woo. Or been put down by her father. Either way, what did I care?

It was late. The PGPS would be closed already for the day so I went straight back to my apartment, an open plan flat that took up the entire top floor in a five-story walkup. Four walls of windows and a huge central sky-dome spanning twenty-odd feet in the middle. I loved it. I'd moved in shortly after Jiji had passed, unable to stomach living in our old home without any remaining family. Now, I removed my muddy boots outside the door, then padded inside to drop my pack on the huge round dining table. The apartment was warm but the air felt cold on my skin. Water had seeped inside the boots and my feet left damp prints on the wood.

Tea first, then a shower and a long soak in my wooden tub. Normally, I'd open every one of the flats fifteen windows to let in fresh air but today it was raining fiercely, Sakura's storms still raging so I didn't dare. I loved the rain, but it definitely belonged outside, not ruining my wood floors.

I turned on the watering system for my indoor garden, an intricate design I'd set up when I'd first moved in that channeled water from a rooftop cistern down through my lemon trees, berry bushes and, rare in any collection on Renga, a life-giving qualitchka vine I'd sprouted as a girl from seed. A gift from Jericha's grandmother when her own had gone to seed, marking the end of sixty attentive years of care.

Remembering Bex's ma'aming, I plucked several large leaves now, covering three in a jar with black seed oil to keep my skin young. The last, I added to a pot of tea – I'd boil some water later. Jericha's grandmother had always credited her weekly cup to her long life and outstanding health – who was I to argue? I'd never called out sick from school or work, so something was working.

I emptied my pack, pulling out the light, dirty pieces of clothes I'd worn over the last week. I'd left the party dress with my cousins for safe-keeping. One less thing to wash, I thought, and brought everything with me over to the bathing area, the only partitioned part of the apartment where a shower and tub stood behind two half-walls. I started filling the tub and stripped down, spending the next twenty minutes using the shower wand to carefully hand-wash my clothes and then my body. Finally, I dumped a pail of cold water over my head, the final rinse, and stepped into the searing heat of the bath.

Perfect.

A long soak, good tea, and a perfectly ripe avocado spritzed with the juice from a Meyer lemon saw my mood much improved. I pulled on a low-key outfit, some shiny black leggings with a thin mesh top, things that would dry easily enough from the rain, and headed out. This wasn't an evening for staying in. Parties weren't my thing, but The Ladybug was different.

The tavern was one of the oldest pubs on the planet, it had been started centuries ago by a band of widows. Word was, the mining company had given them a hefty settlement after some faulty supports had crashed down and killed an entire squad of workers. Some wives had left the planet, but the rest had joined together and put their money to work for them brewing their own beer and serving it up to locals. It had paid off, too. With sister taverns now spanning the planet, all Ladybugs were known as places of refuge and acceptance for kets, a place you could always find a friendly face. The original here in Prime had a reputation for being a hotbed of rebellious, liberal philosophy – no surprise considering the owners' own distrust of corporations and confederacy. Personally, I loved the pub because it hosted readings almost every night, with some of the best poets and storytellers around sharing their verses.

I'd always been obsessed with haiku. Writing poetry was a constant habit of mine, something I did whenever I was idle. I'd write on napkins at restaurants, carve words into sticks in the wild, put a pen to any paper nearby. The lines often flowed from me with barely any concentration, mindless as breathing. Other times, I could spend hours stringing haikus together to form a renga, long-form poetry dating back thousands of years. At the Ladybug, we poets would come together for hours of drinking and poetic styling, each of us taking a turn to link another haiku to the chain of verses, always alternating three-line haiku with two-line verse. Ancient rengas had reached upwards of 10,000 lines composed over days of drinking at bath houses – ambitious and wrinkle-making, surely. I was always happy just to spend a few hours at it.

I climbed the stairs and stepped inside, the heady smell of sweet malt mixing with the comforting pheromones of a hundred warm ket bodies. A young woman was playing a wooden flute on stage, the melody sad and haunting. I shifted the air around me slightly, allowing it to carry the rain from my clothes and skin in a fine mist, rising and dissipating over the room.

"Nikta!" A husky voice called and I looked around, spotting my friends Paisley and Sheila waving from a table near the stage. I'd called the girls just before leaving the house and they'd beaten me here. The flute player glared at me and I shrugged, mouthing "sorry" as I wove through the crowd.

"Ohalo, ladies." I sat down, grinning. A few years my senior, I'd met Paisley through the PGPS and become fast friends with the runner and her wife.

"It's been too long," Sheila chided, wrapping me in a long hug. "You haven't come out in weeks."

"A long spell, even for you," Paisley agreed.

"I know, I know. After all the excitement last month, I needed some downtime."

"I just bet you did," Sheila said, raising a glass. "Pais told me how you got all hot and heavy with Jin's cousin. Must have been ex-haust-ing," she drew out each symbol, fanning herself with one hand.

"That's not what I meant," I laughed.

"Geez, Sheils, I told you she almost died," Paisley hissed.

"Not quite," I said, not wanting to darken the mood. "Anyway, I'm here now!"

"Yes, you are. Drink?" Sheila passed me a shot of something dark and thick and I shook my head. "I'll get it. Need anything?"

"More spring ale?" Paisley held up her empty glass and I grabbed it, knowing the Ladybug liked to refill their draughts to conserve resources, like most establishments in Puraimura. Gal-Con may have had its fingers in every system in the galaxy, but old habits died hard. Our people had worked hard to colonize this planet and even after all these generations, most kets tended towards frugality. Another black mark against us in the eyes of many off-worlders, an oddness of character they just couldn't understand.

Up at the bar, I flagged down the bartender, a quiet girl everyone called Mouse. I had no idea what her real name was, though I was sure she must have one. I also knew she probably wouldn't have worked here if she hadn't been part of the family. Social, she was not. She almost never spoke or met one's eyes, but she could pour a mean drink.

I gave her my order and she twitched her nose, taking Paisley's glass and turning to her task. Someone bumped me and I turned to face a trio of giggling girls.

"Oops, sorry," one said, reaching for a napkin to mop her drink from the bartop.

"You are cut off," laughed one of her friends, poking her in the cheek.

"No! I want to st-"

"Nikta Kozan?" The third friend said, distracting the other two from whatever argument they were about to have. "You went to Cedar Secondary?"

"Yes," I said, wary. The girl looked vaguely familiar, but then the entire trio shared a penchant for heavy makeup and kawaii hair, making it nearly impossible to tell them apart. They could have been one of a hundred girls.

She squealed.

"I knew it! Guys, this is Nikta Kozan! She was three years ahead of us at Cedar." The other two just stared at her, blinking owlishly. I arched an eyebrow, leaning back as she waved a hand over my face, displaying me to her friends like a prize pig. "Kozan? As in Jo-nah?" she drawled.

And suddenly I was surrounded by a trio of screeching owlets, fluffy and wide-eyed. I huffed, rolling my eyes. This was just one of the reasons I had been happy to flee to the woods so often with my grandfather.

"How is he?"

"Does he still swim?

"Is he married?"

This last question set all their heads to nodding vigorously while they looked at me with hope and expectation. I sighed.

"He's good. I don't know if he still swims, I think work keeps him pretty busy. And, unfortunately, he's taken, dating a nice woman named Joyce. Sorry, girls."

"Ohh, lucky," one said, and the others sighed dreamily.

"She must be so happy," another cooed, twirling a long pigtail around one finger.

"Ecstatic, I'm sure." The thing was, I was pretty sure Jonah was the one doing all the work in the relationship. Pretending he was something he wasn't. It was insane, when any girl in Puraimura would have given her left tit to be with him. Which, in itself, I considered demented.

"He was the best swimmer I ever saw," pigtails said.

"The best body I ever saw," another confirmed, then cackled.

"Shut up, you guys," the first girl snapped. "Jonah had substance. He was smart. What's he doing now?"

Though Jonah didn't entirely deserve the edification, I couldn't help raising her up a few notches in my esteem.

"He just made detective on the force in Chalinex. He's very pleased."

"He should be," she said fiercely. "I wanted to curse the entire Olympic team the day I found out they rejected his bid. So what if he was ket? He deserved to be on the team."

"Maybe. But he knew the rules." Mouse returned, slid two beers towards me and accepted the yendars I slipped her in return without a word. The small smirk on her lips when she watched the girls did not escape me, though. There were some things, I thought, that she and I had in common. Or might have, if she'd ever deigned to converse with me.

"Thanks, Mouse!" I called to her retreating figure, already on the move to serve other customers.

She didn't answer, but I caught her smile in the mirror over the bar. I turned back to the girls to find them all staring at me in consternation. Typical. Everyone had worshipped Jonah in high school, idolized him in ways I had never understood. To me, he was always just Jonah. My best friend, the thorn in my side, my annoying little brother. Multi-faceted, yes, but never worthy of a pedestal.

And he had resented me for it. Blamed me for seeing him as anything less than extraordinary: normal, the one thing he'd never, ever wanted to be. Then suddenly, on that fateful day, it had become his greatest aspiration – to be a reg. To leave his ket heritage behind, and move on to the Olympics. But it could never be. Blood never lies. And neither would I.

"Right, well. Enjoy your night, ladies. I'll let Jonah know you said hello." And I escaped with my beers before they realized that I hadn't gotten their names.

I sat down with Sheila and Pais, downed my beer in several long gulps. The night had lost its luster. Behind me, I imagined the three girls whispering and wondering what would become of Jonah; what was wrong with me; how fabulous it must be to be his sister, his lover, his co-worker. When I tried to focus my attention on the stage, I saw Jin singing a lover's ballad and felt the beer sink like lead into my belly. Jin was Kuma's cousin, the impetus behind our meeting. He bore the big bear little resemblance, but his voice held the same timbre. I closed my eyes, remembering the flow of Kuma's verse, the whisper of his breath on my neck. On other parts of my body.

"I can't do this," I whispered, and the involuntary words sent a jolt through me. I needed to move. I needed out of this place. Paisley was leaning towards the stage, entranced by Jin's beautiful melody. Rather than make a big deal of my leaving, I tapped Sheila on the shoulder and whispered in her ear that I had forgotten something I needed to do. "Raincheck? I'll catch up with you guys again soon, I promise."

She frowned, but she must have seen something in my face because she refrained from saying anything other than, "You'd better." She spoke in a hush, blowing me a kiss as she watched me go.

CHAPTER 6

ablution not absolute
starlight, stoke the inner fire

The rain had stopped for the moment but the atmosphere was heavy with the promise of more to come. I started off towards home but changed course after a few blocks, turning down an alley that I knew would lead to the shrine of Amarasu. Formerly the goddess of the Earth Sun, she had evolved over time into the great Star Mother and taken on many of the shining, motherly aspects of the ancient Christian mother, Mary. She was love, she was light, she was compassion. She ruled the heavens and the afterlife and protected her children throughout the universe. She had been my mother's favorite kami, or enlightened being, and tonight I needed that connection.

Below the temple steps, I slowed. I hadn't even realized I'd been running.

Not surprisingly for this hour, I had the temple to myself. Amarasu was the goddess of mothers, and most were home tending their families. But not my mother.

Never again. I removed my shoes and washed my hands in the purification basin just outside the door, using a gleaming moonstone ladle to pour water over each palm. Then, I solemnly clapped twice, bowed and clapped again before striking a large gong to summon Amarasu. Would my mother come as well?

I hoped so. The vibrations of the gong felt like good medicine, and there was no one here to bother so I played it again in a soft series of touches, the rumbling building slowly to a crescendo through my body and soul.

I took a deep breath and felt the spirit of my mother surround me, a warmth that put my spirit at ease.

I kneeled before the smallest statue of Amarasu, the one that had been my mother's favorite. The pregnant ket dressed in a blue gown held her dark arms open as if ready to embrace the petitioner. I envisioned my mother's face in place of Amarasu's and allowed myself to smile.

"Hello, mother," I whispered. "I've missed you. I'm feeling a little bit lost, to tell you the truth. Will you help me find my way?"

There, I'd said it out loud. I wasn't sure if I spoke now to my mother or the star goddess. It didn't matter. In Spirit, they might now be one and the same. Once I'd opened the faucet, the words flowed in earnest and I prayed. For myself, for my path, for Jonah, for Henry.

Henry.

Was that the real reason I had taken on his absence from his family as if it was my own? Was it because I felt lost, like Henry? It was a strange idea. I'd never felt this way before, not for long at any rate. I had always found purpose in my work, peace in the wilds. I had mourned mama, Jiji, even Jonah, but I hadn't felt lost. Had I?

I thought I had been comfortable. Confidant. But the blast at Precinct 8 hadn't just set me on a different course, it had shaken my very foundation. I was still trying to find my center. My people had always believed in the great wheel. Each person was meant to stand in the middle, strongly balanced between air, terra, water, and fire. The center was harmony. The center was strength. The center was spirit.

Where was I?

Too much air, too much water. Thoughts and emotions, raging. Washing away my inner strength, my earth and fire. Terra would take persistent grounding to reclaim, but fire... Fire, I knew how to rebuild. It just needed an act of creation, some joyful activity or passion.

Immediately, Kuma sprang to mind and I realized what I'd been missing. Not the man, surely. But the fire. He'd lit it within me, replenished the well when it had been low. He'd appeared amidst the crisis, and returned me to center. And then he'd left.

I didn't miss him. I didn't. He was temporary, and as such utterly replaceable. Like Yuki's white lunar orb overhead, his transit had been short and erratic. Nothing to plan a life around. I heard the giggles of a young couple, flirting in the entrance as they washed each other's hands. Here to ask for the blessing of a child, I guessed. And suddenly, I felt like Amarasu had sent me a sign and I knew just what to do. Love was indeed everywhere; it was in me. I didn't need to go far to find it and I certainly didn't need to look anywhere outside of myself.

Rising, I nodded to the couple and exited the temple, giving up the space so they could supplicate in private. I'd been lost, but now I knew where to go. I stalked east, back through the entertainment district, past The Ladybug and The Iron Axe, The Hammer and The Watering Hole. Drinks, food, company. I didn't need anything so refined. Dancing, hard and fast, that was what I sought. Dancing, and the hungry fire that went with it.

I bypassed the line in the street and winked at the bouncer as I walked right into The Kabuki. The club had a long and varied history, having started as a traditional theatre, enjoyed a brief stint as a seedy cabaret, and then morphed into a wild dance club. The rules here were simple: dance hard, don't pass out, no fights and no magic. The last was often overlooked, as long as the magic didn't involve violence upon another person. The bouncer was familiar, Maeve's youngest son Jimmy Lewis. He'd been working the door on and off for the last year. Even if our mothers hadn't been old friends, he would have let me in – all the bouncers here knew me, just as they knew their bosses loved it when I came and put on a show.

The air inside was pulsing with the vibrations of the music, the hairs on my head registering every bass beat. A trio of drummers pounded out a deep tribal rhythm while the melody set by string quartet seemed to race the vocalist's arias rife with operatic intensity. I recognized the words of Carmina Burana, one of my favorites. Another message from Amarasu? Most of the words in the opera had been written thousands of years ago in tribute to the Queen of Aquitaine, a celebration of her "Court of Love."

Love, indeed, I thought and smiled. My mother had often said there were no coincidences, only synchronicities. When I'd asked her once what the difference was, she'd said one was a sign of Spirit's love for us, the other its absence. And because Spirit could never truly be absent, only one could exist.

Now, I understood and the knowledge filled me with power. Power, raging for release.

Which was, of course, why I'd come here.

I felt the air around me shift, the hair on my ears lifting in anticipation. I approached the bouncer by the stage who only needed to take one look at the auric glow beginning to coalesce near my skin before he moved aside and gestured for me to go ahead. A smile danced in his eyes and I knew he would be hard-pressed in the coming minutes to watch the crowd instead of the stage.

I ignored the stairs and mounted the stage in one agile leap, winking at the back-up singers as I positioned myself nearby. I wouldn't block the other performers, I knew there were many who had come to see them, just as I knew that the three boys running out the door would be pounding down the street announcing the coming show and bringing in a crowd to see Nikta Kozan put on a show. This was why the bouncers let me in – the bar would make more tonight in door fees than they did on any other.

I took a deep breath, allowed the cello to thrum through me, the frenetic viola to fuel the fire in my soul, and began.

I sank into horse stance and raised my right hand to shoulder level, scooping up air and breathing light into it. Green flame erupted, a fire that would not consume, and I twirled one finger, sending the writhing mass upwards where it took form as winged panther chasing its own tail. I shifted to the side, dropped my left hand in one fluid motion and manifested another swirl of fire and wind, a vibrant blue dragon to twine itself between my legs. Sleepy, at first. Peaceful. I rolled my neck, then picked up the pace, passing through several complicated Qigong forms. The dragon countered each of my moves as a dance. And slowly, ever so slowly, it grew from the size of a small, slithering dog to that of a horse, rearing up its head, unfolding its own wings to bring its head level with my own. I grabbed its head between my hands and kissed its brow, then lifted my hands and in a shower of aqua sparks sent it skyward, rising, rising, to meet its love in the air.

I laughed, ecstatic, dancing and twirling as the panther wriggled its haunches and pounced, rolling with the dragon and beginning a cosmic game of chase. The crowd oohed and ahhed, and many of the observers' own auras began to spark and glow, so that the entire floor began to take on the look of the sky, a misty collection of nebulae, stars and galaxies. And wasn't that all we were? Stars and souls, intertwined?

The music picked up tempo and so did my show. I sent my spirit animals into a circle dance, allowing them to take on the shape of humans dancing their power as my ancestors had before me. The backup singers took their cue from me, harmonizing the words of love with those of the opera.

May the stars lift your sadness.

May your heart fill with love.

We are a circle

Dancing both ways.

Yes, I thought. They understood. Haiku had long been my refuge, a way to sift through my feelings and thoughts. But here, tonight? The magic was a way to let Spirit speak in my stead.

Indeed, the magic had taken on a life of its own, drawing on the crowd as much as from my own connection to the elements. The energy, rather than feeling foreign, filled me up. *This was home.* This was love. All of it. All of us.

And then, on the tail of that thought, I watched a new animal leap into the air, a dark horse rimmed with fire. Someone trying to steal the show, or join it? The horse circled my spirit dancers, running swiftly between them to leave a trailing flame, a vermillion figure eight burning brightly which my dancers now traced, before it turned its sights on me. Hooves pounding soundlessly, kicking up flame, it rushed at me. I had no time to think, only brace myself for impact, choosing to trust the love that surrounded me rather than give in to any fear. Three, two, one... the horse ran through me, around me, into me. Coursed through my veins and I tasted its magic, identified the maker.

Innis. I sighed his name and let the ecstasy take me, laughing, dancing. I should have known my sometimes lover might be here, cousins as he was with Jimmy. The music was building now, and I had no choice but to join it, watch it. The crowd was going wild, and so was our display. One of my dancers had leapt onto the stallion's back to ride out above the heads of the audience, a drum in one hand showering fireworks onto them each time it was beaten in time with the music. The other had reclaimed its dragon form and reared up behind the main vocalist, wings wide open, head thrown back, breath of green fire keeping time with her song.

Innis McRory leaped onto the stage to take me in his arms, swinging me into our own heated circle dance. For me, a dance of spirit. For Innis? Well, he'd been pursuing me for years, always taking what he could. What I would give him. His family was my family, his aunt like a second mother to me. I'd always tried to keep him at arm's-length, but there was only so much I could do. He was, after all, a McRory. Tall, dark, handsome. A sorcerer with his hands, both in and out of bed. I'd never wanted to be boxed into a relationship, but I had needs, physical needs that Innis always knew just what to do with. For him, tonight, I could see it was a dance of passion, perhaps even love. And, gods help me, I knew I wouldn't be able to turn him away. I could never turn him away. Somehow, despite my best intentions to separate lust from friendship, from family ties, I always let him back into my bed.

When we made it that far. The last time I'd seen we'd made do with the relative privacy of a quiet balcony at his aunt's birthday party.

"McRory," I breathed in his ear when he pulled me close. "You're stealing my show."

"Fair's fair, isn't it? After all, you've stolen my heart."

"Shh," I said, and placed a finger over his lips, dancing backwards. Just as I would have moved out of reach, he grasped my hand and reeled me back in. The song soared and the crowd roared. And then, all was still. The song had ended. Our totems rode back to us and exploded in a burst of light, streaming back into our bodies. My back arched with the power of it, pushing me deeper into his arms and he caught me. Like always. Innis always knew how to catch me.

"Someday, Nikta, I'll keep you, too," he whispered, and I wondered if he'd read my mind or if I'd said part of the words out loud. Before I could chastise him for this public display, rumors of which I was just now realizing would almost certainly get back to his family – to Maeve and Maury, dammit – he sprang off the stage the way only a ket could, landing twenty feet away.

The crowd parted, letting him leave, and he walked straight to the exit without another glance. All swagger. "I've got you now," it seemed to say.

"Like hell," I said, but it came out in more of a purr than a snarl and I couldn't help blushing as all eyes returned to me.

Quickly, I linked hands with the singers and led them in a bow. As the crowd applauded at length, calling for encores, I hugged the musicians. I thanked them for letting me share the stage and then I escaped to the back of the club, leaving out the back door. It slammed behind me and I collapsed against the cool brick of the building, desperately trying to slow my pulse.

I'd started the night wanting to forget Kuma, come to the club looking to vent my power and express my independence, to cement my blessings from Amarasu, and I'd received... what?

Innis McRory, that was what.

Tara's toes, what could the gods be thinking?

CHAPTER 7

drooping flower nods
it knows more than you or I
hush! this song has words

Senses heightened, thoughts whirling, I went home knowing that I would never be able to sleep. I tried to banish all thoughts of Innis and Kuma from my head, but even my worries about Henry weren't enough to distract me for long.

A night like this called for my mother's night potion.

A blend of dreamless poppy, lavender, and kavakaa thrice blessed by Yuki's light – an irregular moon for irregular thoughts. A few drops would relax the muscles and mind. A few more would send me into a deep sleep, thanks to the dreamless poppy, the bright and wild cousin of the opioid poppies so many had fought over millennia ago. Now, those poppies had been eradicated, burned from the planets in an effort to contain the addictions. It didn't matter – new drugs surfaced all the time. Some better, some worse than the old ones. But dreamless poppy was safe and just what I needed to put my racing hormones to rest.

I slept for twelve hours, awakened refreshed and at peace. Renga's most irregular of moons, Yuki had set, taking all my cares with her. *Men. Who needed them?*

I was an independent woman, and there was work to do. I threw off the covers, ate a quick meal of fruit and smoked fish, and jogged over to the PGPS offices.

Paisley wasn't at her post today, someone new manning security at the back gates. Even if she had been, the process to gain admittance had become more stringent now that the mail had been infiltrated the month before by a bomber. After several minutes of sniffing and inspection, I was allowed to head straight to Florence Green, Sorting Master and Manager of the Carry with Care Program. She'd carried for years, been trained by my very own Jiji. At sixty, she was like a grandmother to me. Or a very fit and fierce auntie.

Seeing me now, she squealed and threw her arms around me in a choking hug. Normally, Florence prided herself on professionalism and restraint, but ever since I'd almost become shrapnel she'd allowed herself to be more demonstrative at work. She drew back, trailing one of her razor-sharp nails to trail down my cheek. She filed them nightly, a defensive habit from trail-running that she'd never abandoned.

"You can stop examining me, Flo," I laughed, pushing past her to dump my latest haul on her table. A flurry of mailing tubes and carefully wrapped packages drummed melodically against the wooden surface.

"Never," she vowed, a twinkle in her eye. "I promised your family I would watch out for you, remember?" She tapped her nails against my forehead and stepped back to her table. "I'm glad you're here. I have things for you."

"A carrier's work is never done," I said.

"No, not that. I mean, yes, I've already sorted for your route, that bin's yours. But I meant these. They came in yesterday by regular post." She handed me two small missives – a single rolled piece of thick paper, secured with plain tape, and a delicate wax-sealed envelope made of translucent rice paper.

I examined them both. The first had no return address and I guessed it was probably junk mail: a new restaurant opening or a local sale. The latter bore the mark of the Enso. Curious, I tore open the second envelope and scanned the contents. It was a formal acknowledgment of the help I had given the Enso the month before in Chalinex City, complete with an honorary registration with their chapter. This was unusual since I was already under the auspices of my hometown chapter here in Prime. I was sure my cousins had arranged the extra protection – and protection it surely was, since each month the Enso performed special rituals calling in the elements to bolster the strength and health of their local members. Now, I would be doubly blessed.

I showed Flo, who clucked appreciatively. "It's only right, I suppose, after everything you went through. Your grandfather would be proud to see you moving up in the world already. So young, and so much promise. We always agreed on that."

"You always agreed on everything," I reminded her.

"Indeed, we did." She chuckled. "Now, what are your plans while you're in town? How about we get some dinner later?"

"I can't. I'm heading back out." The words were said before I'd even known I'd made a decision.

"What?" she said in surprise, watching me gather the mail for delivery and stuff it into my pack. There was a lot there; one package so big I realized I'd have to carry a second shoulder sling just to accommodate it. "You're heading back out already?"

"Yeah, think so." Truth was, I was restless. The magic show with Innis had me shook and I didn't want to stick around to find out why.

Florence looked at me deeply, her pupils going wide for a moment, then she nodded. "Man troubles."

It wasn't a question.

I exhaled heavily and she patted my shoulder.

"The wilds are just the place to be, then. You'll find your way, I have no doubt." She kissed me on each cheek. "Safe travels, Nikta."

"Thanks, Flo," I said, wrapping her in a hug.

I tucked my own two letters inside my sweater, looped my pack over my shoulders and picked up the large package. Whatever it was, it was light. Normally the Carry with Care unit had a weight and size limit – someone had paid beaucoup bucks to get a box this size through the sorting. Hand-drawn artwork done in several hands, young and old, beautified the plain brown paper. The washi tape was gold and glittering, and bright silk flower petals had been taped to the top, though they'd already begun to fade. Someone was cared for, the package said. Someone was loved.

I promised Florence we'd get together when I returned and I walked home through the markets, picking up trail food and a new notebook made of thin, barely-there rice paper. The pages had a transient feeling, like my poems, and I liked the idea of their impermanence. I picked up a set of copper- and silver-inked pens, too, the idea of their impending shimmer on the delicate pages pleasing me, like starlight and moonlight descending into speech. Into patterns and rhythms.

At home, I repacked my bag, made room for the new implements and a change of clothes – bare whispers of fabric, the most I could fit. Most of my clothes were thin, easy to wash, light to carry. Good for the trail. I ate a warm meal of fresh rice and bean curd, opened a jar of strawberry preserves for dessert and indulged in the sticky sweetness. The phone rang and I licked my spoon, lingering a moment before answering.

"Hallo?"

"Kozan, that you? Lyric Pearce here."

"Detective, ohalo." Even though there was no one here to see me, I wiped my mouth and straightened my spine, holding the phone cord in one hand while the other tightened around the earpiece. "I was just about to head over your way. What can I do for you?"

CHAPTER 8

*whispers tell many stories
yet none have tales worth hearing*

"Nothing at the moment." He sounded annoyed and my hackles rose, unbidden.

"Then why-"

"Henry Gunjabmi never left Hokku. There is no record of him boarding any ship."

I sank into a chair. Outside, Hokku was low in the sky, getting ready to set. Its small, pale blue orb had never looked lonelier.

I tried to make sense of what Lyric was saying.

"He's still on the moon?"

"No."

"I don't understand. If he didn't leave, he must be there. Did they look everywhere?" I insisted.

"Believe me Nikta, the galactic police scoured that base from top to bottom. As you must know, all interstellar trading posts and moon bases are considered GalCon territory, and as such they are run very tightly. Everyone on the base must be accounted for, because otherwise they would run into aeration issues."

"Yes, but if he didn't leave?" I let the question's implication hang between us, unspoken.

"I know." I could hear Lyric exhale in frustration and for the first time it dawned on me that this wasn't the second, or even third, conversation he had held on this topic. His next words confirmed my suspicions. "I've been on the phone with Hokku's commander five times today. Three yesterday. I asked the same questions as you. Unfortunately, I didn't get too many answers. The ones I did get, I don't think you're going to like."

I swallowed. "What do we know? They don't think he wandered outside, do they?" Never having been terraformed, the atmosphere on Hokku was negligible. I knew the station offered walking tours, but without the proper equipment a ket would die within hours. A reg? They'd been known to last fifty minutes before succumbing to the conditions. Henry couldn't have been that stupid. I swore, imagining that maybe he had, and missed part of what Lyric was saying.

"-think so. The exits are all video monitored and biometrically sealed so they can't be opened by just anyone."

"Then what? How does someone just go missing like that? Please tell me they don't think he fell down a waste pipe."

Lyric chuckled and I relaxed in spite of myself. "Again, not likely. Though of course those, ahem, exits are unmonitored." Lyric sighed, became serious again. "GalCon doesn't like to admit this, their security at the moon base is supposed to be top-rate, but I've come to know the commander there pretty well." He trailed off, silence stretching between us awkwardly.

"And?" I finally demanded. "What is it you don't want to tell me, Lyric? What the hell is going on up there?" Over the line, I heard Lyric exhale loudly, could practically *feel* the air brush my neck, and all my senses suddenly went on alert. "Dammit, what?"

"There are rumors. Nothing's been proven and officially, it's not happening, but...my guy believes there are slavers operating through the base. People, mostly young, attractive people, are disappearing. They arrive, but no one knows where they go. The Gunjabmi's aren't the first family to come looking for answers. The problem, though, is that the logbooks don't match up. There are no records of these kids leaving the moon but it's clear they aren't there, either."

"Are you sure? How do we know they aren't hidden in some brothel or something?"

"Impossible. The air is carefully monitored, every body on the base has to be accounted for, factored into the life support generators, otherwise they'd run into problems. Still, I had the same doubts you did, made them run the numbers. Twice. The base is clear."

"Well, then, what? Henry is gone? Sold off to some pervert or salt mine light-years away? What the hell am I supposed to tell his family?"

"I can't tell you that. But it might not be as bad as all that. It's a lot harder to smuggle things into space than it is to send them back to Renga off the books. GalCon customs runs its checks on goods coming in and going out – Hokku is basically considered a Rengan outpost. But ships on their way back down to us, you know how they are. Ancient workhorses, run by the same guys day in and day out. No one questions their logs, no one checks their holds."

"Maybe they should start," I grumbled.

"Believe me, changes are coming. GalCon always proceeds carefully, though, you know that. They don't like to infringe on planetary matters."

"So basically, this is our problem, GalCon out?"

"For now."

And there it was.

"I can't tell the Gunjabmi's this story. We don't even know what's happened. It's worse than not knowing, isn't it?" I asked.

"It's not the kind of thing that helps a body sleep at night, no. I've looked at it every way I can. I even thought about going up to Hokku myself." For a moment, my spirit rose. Surely Lyric could find something his friend had missed. His next words brought me back to earth. "Unfortunately, that would cause more trouble than good. If I go up there poking around I'd be stepping on GalCon's toes. It might piss them off enough to move faster, but it might have the opposite effect. Worse, I could inadvertently tip off the slavers. Look, I know it's hard to wait and do nothing, but I think that's just what we need to do. If we play our cards too early the slavers could suspend operations."

"So?" I asked wildly. "Isn't that what we want?"

"We *want*," Lyric emphasized the word, "to find Henry. To find everyone who's disappeared. We can't let them erase the trail."

"Assuming there is a trail."

"Assuming, yes."

Now, it was my turn to exhale. "I don't like it."

"I know," he said. "I don't like it either. I'm sorry, Nikta. I really did try."

"I know. Thank you, Lyric. You'll let me know if you have any updates?"

"Of course. We're not giving up. We need to let GalCon run with it for a while on their end. In the meantime, I've pulled some cold cases, checking for similarities. Hopefully, something will turn up soon."

"Gods willing," I murmured.

"Yes. Prayers can't hurt, either," he said, paused. "What will you tell the family?"

"What can I tell them? He's missing. That's all. They don't need to know where he might be, not until we know where he isn't. Family worries, you know? They imagine all the worst things."

"I know," he said, and I believed he did. How would he act, I wondered, if it was his wife, his children? Would he still sit tight, pore over cold cases? Or would he be on Hokku already, scanning every surface? I shook my head. It wasn't right to second-guess Lyric, not now when he was acting like a real human, with real feelings. "Tell them… tell them I am on the case. Tell them we have everyone searching. For better or worse, we will find Henry."

It was a vow I knew he might not be able to keep. Still. "I'll hold you to that," I said.

"I know," he repeated quietly and hung up.

CHAPTER 9

hearts of ghosts stalking
things forgotten, discovered
leaving oaths behind

The heavy pink orb of Sakura had finally set, taking our ancestors and gods with her for thirteen days of rest. The sky glimmered darkly overhead, though Yuki was making a short visit to lend her auspicious blessings to the day of Harai – purification rituals and celebrations to bless our ancestors as they traveled back to the skyworld. The moon shone like her namesake in the sky, a ball of snow round and pure; not that I'd ever seen such chilly marvels here.

I'd made tracks right after the detective's call. The land was my real home, the truest balm to my spirit. Or, it always had been. I'd made camp early and spent the evening by the fire engraving sticks with poems and prayers. A prayer for my mother. An ode to Jiji, Jonah, father. Haiku for the Gunjabmi's. Blessings to Kuma, Jericha, my cousins. Prayers upon prayers, my pile of sticks grew throughout the night. I fell asleep with my knife in my hand, a poem half-etched. When I woke, Yuki was rising and our ancestors had gone. I stoked the fire, set water to boiling in a pot surrounded by coals, prepared a cup with leaves of lemon and hips of rose. I gathered the sticks into my arms and began to dance slowly around the fire, shuffling to my left, blessing the ancestors on their journey in a ghost dance as my mother had taught me to do. With every ring around the fire marked by Yuki in my sights, I tossed a stick upon the flames. A prayer for my parents. A blessing for my brother. Questions for my heart. Stick after stick, the fire burned, the prayers shapeshifted into smoke rising heavenward.

Finally, my arms were empty and I danced with abandon. By the time I was done, my tea-water had boiled itself half away, leaving enough for a single cup of tea. I poured the water over into my travel mug and shed my sweater, warmed by my celebratory rounds. I set it beside me, folding it, and noticed the letters I'd tucked inside one day earlier. *Stupid*, I thought. I should have left the Enso registration at home in my safe. Oh well. There wasn't much I could do about it now, other than store it inside a more secure pocket in my pack. As for the other, I flipped the single rolled of taped paper in my hand, catching it deftly. This would make good tinder at my next campsite. One shouldn't always rely on magic, after all.

Half-curious, waiting for my tea to cool, I slit open the mail with one fingernail. Expected a restaurant announcement, a curio sale.

Received a poem.

Kitten,

> *i walk for miles in wilds empty and still*
> *stumble over rocks, suckle rivers sweet*
> *feet calloused, muscles strong, and heart yet ill*
>
> *love wanders not, pushes instead, insists*
> *i must go where my heart is denied, masked*
>
> *love! don't you wonder what treasure is lost?*
> *this thing buried is the hardest to find*
> *a shining stone sleeps blanketed with moss*
>
> *blankets, sodden and steaming, i throw off*
> *in the night, moaning, missing, i sleep rough*
>
> *waking, finding not love but stars to guide*
> *through wilds tamed, each step brings understanding*
> *the treasure is i and nothing gold hides*
>
> *in missing you i have found myself, still*

Yours,
Kokuma Matsui
Kyogamura

What the hell was this? A love letter? A good-bye? The Elysienne sonnet read like a rebuke, passion bitter in the mouth, yet he signed it "yours." What game was he playing? Disgusted, I held the roll of rough paper over the fire, willed myself to burn it.

Could not.

I told myself it would be a waste to burn such a good piece of good tinder. Slipped the letter back into my pocket. Resolved to forget it and found myself reading it again minutes later. And again. Finally, I crumpled it in my hand, decided to rid myself of the cursed thing.

And yet.

Instead of burning it, I tamped out the fire and doused it with the rest of my tea. The letter found its way back into my keeping, this time in my pack with that of the Enso. I had mail to deliver. Enough of this madness, I told myself, and headed out at full speed, dodging trees and leaping from boulder to boulder, making my own way, my own trail. The wilds were my own treasure and nothing, no one, could take that from me.

I traversed two hills, three mountains, and still, I ran. I forged a river and circumvented a swamp. The homesteading woman I handed the huge box to sank to her knees on the floor of her front porch, weeping tears of joy and thanking me for bringing her the carefully chosen souvenirs from her husband and youngest children: things for each of their teenage daughters, for her. The mail had been delayed, of course. He and the younglings had been traveling far across the reaches of GalCon to visit his parents and had found little access to PGPS offices, but the presents had come and it called for a celebration. Missy, Sara, and Susan bade me stay the night, eat smoked pork and cake with them, play a low-stakes game of mah-jongg, drink plum wine. It was late, so I agreed.

The next morning, I left my winnings and a haiku written in thanks on the dining table. I slipped out early, long before the rest of the household rose. A night of celebration, followed by a morning of rest. It was the least they deserved. Me, I had more to do. Three packages had come in for the Night Seekers, a small religious group living a half day's run from here.

It was an easy trek following Hot Creek through verdant valleys. The narrow waterway ran for almost a hundred miles, sulphur-laden steam rising from its surface, the water heated by subterranean vents almost the entire way. At lunchtime, only a few clicks from my destination, I decided to stop for a quick bath in one of the creek's pools. The warm water worked magic on my muscles, its mineral content softening, soothing. I closed my eyes and sank all the way in, allowing the water to close over my head. Ten...Twenty...Forty...Fifty...Sixty...Ninety. Ninety-one. I allowed myself to rise, slowly, and drew the humid air deeply into my lungs. I shook out my hair and leaned back, reaching over into my pack for a tin of trail mix to sate my hunger. I watched a trio of night herons draw close to the pool on the other side, their beaks testing the water, looking for pupfish.

The Night Seekers had chosen their location wisely, claiming a stretch of land alongside one of the creek's largest, deepest pools. Though well known in Prime as a holy place for ritual bathing and healing, no one had ever tried to claim the territory around Aligna's Well for themselves before. I wasn't sure what the seeker's spiritual mission was but they had quickly built twenty co-op houses centered around a central temple hall adjacent to the pool. When they'd arrived the year before I hadn't asked what or who they worshipped, and they hadn't tried to convert me. I'd appreciated their restraint, though I'd suspected it had something more to do with the whispers of witchcraft I caught whenever I visited than any godly manners. I'd told the Enso in Puraimura about them – an apprentice had made a notation in a large book but not seemed overly interested in the settlement. Renga was, after all, built on premises of tolerance, freedom, and exploration, regardless of what some of our newer citizens might have preferred.

My fingernails scraped against the bottom of the now-empty tin and I sighed, feeling both satisfied and lazy. If I spent any longer in the pool I'd probably fall asleep and that wouldn't do. It was too open here, too unprotected, and I had precious cargo to look after. I rose from the pool, ruffling my hair with my fingers to shake some of the water out and pulled on a clean flesh-toned bralette and underwear. My leggings stuck in places to my damp legs but I was relaxed enough not to mind. Finally, I donned a barely-there crocheted tunic of brown silk and my travel sweater.

Time to check on the godlies, as my father had always called the various troupes of fanatics who came to Renga looking for redemption in the wilds. Mama had shushed him time and again, but Pa hadn't been the type to go to honor the ancestors at Harai or visit the temples during festivals. Pragmatic, sarcastic, Pa had always believed life was about what you could see and touch. He'd shied from using his magic, preferred fighting with his fists to hurling a ball of flame. He was the one who'd trained me in the martial arts, and it was him Jiji had once blamed for Jonah's reg appearance.

"Tom denies who he is, won't use magic. And look what that has wrought," he'd yelled at my mother once. "Look at your son! He forgets who he is because he's been born looking like someone else!" I don't know what had brought on the argument, but the words had frozen Jonah and I mid-stride outside the kitchen doorway, returning from school. My mother sucked in her breath, ordered him from the kitchen with a hiss. Jiji had not visited for months after that, not until our father's funeral. A runner in his twenties, Pa had quit the PGPS when we were little to open a mixed martial-arts training center. To stay near Jonah and me, he'd always said, ruffling our hair. Then, one day at the pub some guys had been harassing a couple of young girls. Cornering them in the back near the bathrooms, it was said. My father had stepped in, put up his hands instead of a shield. And he'd been taken down in a double blast of fire and ice, magic and fury. The girls had been saved, the thugs arrested.

My father's back, broken when he hit the wall. He died three days later in the hospital, as much from devastation as anything else.

After that, I'd spent more time than ever with Jiji in the wilds and Jonah had thrown himself into his training as a swimmer. Training, as Jiji had said, as if he wasn't a ket, as if he could someday be an Olympic medalist. No one had warned him away from his hopes or dreams. No one had had the heart to stop him. The pragmatist in the family had died, and the rest of us were just trying to survive without him.

I shook my head, trying to expel the memories. Too much sadness there. Too much loss. It was always too easy to dive into the downward spiral such miseries invited. I was here now, in the majestic frontier, under nebulas of wonder, and I was alive. This world, my father would have said, was a blessing of life. I had to take its gifts with both hands and never look back. I drove myself into a sprint, the wet hair on my head cooling in the wind, then drying. When I approached the compound of the Night Seekers, I slowed. In the month since I'd been here, they'd been busy. A tight wall of wooden spikes rose chest high and a gatehouse had been erected next to the worn dirt path.

I slowed to a jog, watched the guard unwind himself from his seat to stand. I noted the cache of arrows slung over the back of the chair, the bow leaning against the wall. His hand strayed towards his belt where it came to rest on the wooden hilt of a large curved dagger.

"Hi," I smiled, coming to a halt several yards away. Slowly, I raised a hand and flashed my PGPS bracelet. "I have deliveries for Roana Claus and David Warren."

"Packages? You can leave them here with me. Entry is for seekers and paying human pilgrims only." He gestured at a large box on a table to his left where a sign had been elegantly painted demanding ten yendar for pilgrims, thirty for use of the pool. *Humans only*, someone had scrawled underneath in a rougher hand.

"Thirty yendar to use Aligna's Well? That's a bit steep, considering it's public water," I scoffed.

"Public water, maybe, but the land surrounding it has been legally claimed. If one wants to enter the pool, they'll have to cross our land," he said flatly.

"No thanks. Any magic in the pool is surely hiding now that you're around. But I will be needing access to the people I named. My deliveries must be signed for."

"No."

"No?" I repeated, bristling. "You dare deny a special carrier entry?"

"Not my rules." He shrugged. "Kets are unnatural, unclean in the eyes of the old gods. Letting you on our land is considered an offense. There is nothing we want that had been touched by the likes of you. Leave the tainted packages and be gone."

"I won't do any such thing," I said, my voice rising. "PGPS! Special deliveries for Roana Claus and David Warren!" I called out loudly.

He stared at me, unmoved.

"PGPS!"

Quickly, the gate swung open and woman emerged looking annoyed. "What is this noise?" she asked the guard, barely sparing me a glance. "She disturbs our prayers."

"I'm sorry. It's this creature. She wants to deliver a package to Roana."

The woman paled, then looked me over more carefully from my bracelet to my ears. Her nose wrinkled in distaste. "You may give the packages to me. I am Megain, I oversee these seekers."

"I will do no such thing. The recipients must sign in person. It's a silly PGPS rule, you know, but what can I do? I have to follow GalCon law."

The implication, of course, was that she was breaking several here. Claiming public water? Barring kems from entry? Forget PGPS regulations, the Enso would have her head for breaking with the rule of law.

She didn't flinch.

"Fine," I said, gritting my teeth. "I'll go. Just know that as an operative of both the Enso and the CCPD, I will be filling out numerous reports on the violations here today."

Megain crossed her arms defiantly over her chest. "So now the police work hand-in-hand with the unclean? Good to know. You may go."

For a moment, I considered blasting her. Unclean indeed. I'd show her unclean. A shower of mud from the banks of the creek would surely wipe that smug look off her face. A strong breeze rose around us, dusting them with debris from the trail. The seekers stood their ground, but I saw the guard begin to unsheathe his knife. I remembered my father's teachings. Fists over magic, patience over anger. Never start a fight you don't intend to end.

I forced myself to unclench my fists and took a step backward. "Consider yourselves warned."

I turned my back on the pair, retreating slowly, but not before raising an invisible shield.

I didn't trust Megain or her goon not to shoot me in the back. My chest burned, but not from any magical effort or strain; nor was it this group's prejudice that pained me. I'd never had to abandon a delivery before and somehow the failure stung worse than any arrow.

CHAPTER 10

starving, hunger makes strange friends
searching for answers in clouds

I ran through the rest of my deliveries on auto-pilot, barely remembering to smile. Kuma's poem remained an enigma, Innis a maddening distraction, and the Night Seekers had dug under my skin like a thorn. I was frustrated. I was hurt. I was confused. I didn't want to be any of those things, so I tried to simply be zen. No thoughts. No feelings.

I sucked at being zen.

Not that anyone seemed to notice or care. I dropped off four letters and five small parcels, all of them marked *Carry with Care*, all of them met with wide smiles and eager hands. All of them clasped to chests, received with thanks, and torn into before I hit the streets.

I saved the best for last, an-off world letter for Lady Nestra Laroche. I knew her, knew her kind. Haughty, beautiful, and always seeking, always hunting for a way to make her mark, to prove herself. The last time I'd seen her, she'd been high on the feed, addicted to the magical hallucinogenic. I'd been working with the CCPD to find the source of the feed and we'd succeeded in taking down the main producer. Weeks had passed and I wondered how Nestra was faring without access to the dreamy drug. The feed had had a way of putting you in the middle of your fantasies – making out with the object of your crush, playing in your favorite wonderland, feeling firsthand what it would be like to have all your wildest dreams come true. Some hard-core users had needed to check into mental health facilities when the drug had vanished from the streets, depression hitting hard as their dreams faded.

I got it. Reality was no picnic.

But Nestra Laroche? I wasn't sure what she had to be sad about. Her dad was Vice Consul Tindare of the Spartan Legions of Earth. Nestra herself was the widow of Lord Aganon Laroche. By any world's standards, she had more money than she could spend in three lifetimes – and she'd chosen to bring it here. Renga, where two Galactic Credits could buy you five Yendar. Renga, where tech was useless and living was cheap. She'd stuck her fingers in a hundred pots, taking over nightclubs, investing in businesses throughout the city, doubling her wealth by the month if one could believe in the local gossips. Yet, I knew she missed her home. The rainbows, blue skies and sunshine. Like so many daughters before her, her investment in Renga seemed to be nothing more than a desperate attempt to gain her daddy's approval – approval she would probably never enjoy.

I'd been lucky. I'd had a loving family, a good father. But I knew how she felt. Was I any different, putting myself in harm's way and working with the CCPD just to be near Jonah, to win my twin's affection?

I knew I wasn't. So I tolerated the questioning by her guards, tried not to roll my eyes when they insisted on accompanying me across the yard. When her butler Oxby opened the door and narrowed his eyes at me, blasting me yet again for refusing to use the servants' entrance, I simply grinned and showed him my bracelet, reminding him that only Lady Nestra could sign for the mail I carried.

Grumbling, the old coot led me down the hall to a room that reminded me of the Grecian pleasure houses from old texts. Pillows lined the floor, the ceiling was painted a brilliant azure blue dotted with fluffy white clouds and colorful curtains billowed from open windows four times my height. Amid the opulence, Nestra Laroche reclined, reading. Her hair was messier than usual, the hip-length dark strands gathered into messy braids atop her head. Oxby cleared his throat and Nestra peered at him over a glittering pair of emerald-encrusted reading glasses.

"Madame, forgive the intrusion but-" Oxby broke off abruptly when Nestra raised a hand imperiously. She was staring at me, her expression unreadable.

"Leave us, Oxby."

Startled, he glared at me but did as he was told, closing the doors behind me as I stepped inside.

"Lady Laroche," I began.

"You have something for me?" she asked, looking hopeful. Suddenly, I realized that she must mean the feed. The last time I'd seen her, I'd brought her several doses – the last she'd ever see, I imagined.

"Yes, a letter," I said, striding forward and drawing the off-world missive from my bag. Tightly rolled and marked with an official GalCon seal, it looked important. "You just need to sign for it, here."

I shoved my notepad in her face but she took the tube from my other hand and blinked up at me with large, sad eyes. The kohl-rimmed orbs glistened with unshed tears and whatever I might have said died on my lips.

"Will you sit with me?" she asked, pulling me down beside her before I could object.

"Really, ma'am, I should be going. If you'll just-"

But she wasn't listening. She had turned the tube in her hands, scanned the writing. Now, her lips twisted into a snarl. Her voice shifted to near-song, disturbing and hollow. "Papa wants a word with me." Long, pointed nails pried the tube open, unrolled the letter within. "Papa knows what's best." Then she glanced up at me, eyes glittering like a snake about to strike. "Papa can go to hell."

I cleared my throat, leaned back. "Ahem. Okay. Well, I should really be going..."

She sprang up and began to pace. "He thinks he can tell me how to run my businesses? Businesses I built with my own money? Just because he sold me to that drunken sod, Aganon, he thinks he gets a say in my life? Well, screw him! I'm free now, dammit. I don't have to listen to anyone, or do anything, if I don't want to." She skewered me with a glance. "Isn't that right!?"

"Absolutely. We take freedom very seriously here on Renga. It's what we're known for."

"Yes, it is, isn't it?" She agreed, looking mollified. Sane, almost. One of her braids had fallen and she twisted it in her hands now the way a washwoman might wring a towel, or a henchman might cinch a noose. "It's why I came here. The freedom. I can be anything here. Anyone. I mean, who's going to stop me? A ket, like you?" She laughed. "No, your kind knows only too well what it means to be free."

If she was trying to gain my sympathy, she was going about it the wrong way. But her words about freedom sparked an idea.

"That's true. Ever since the mines closed, we have done all we can to make this a truly free world," I agreed.

"You have! Renga is known throughout the Confederation as one of a handful of places that is still truly wild, truly free." She rushed back to my side, collapsed beside me with eyes bright and shining.

"Too wild, maybe. The law here is weak. And some people...well, some people don't fare as well as others."

"A necessary evil, some would say," she commiserated. "But I try to take care of as many as I can. You've met my guard, Clive?" I nodded. "He was abused. Taken advantage of. I took him under my wing and now he has security. Happiness."

And you, I thought, have the run of a private club previously open only to men. I knew she had found the ignorant weasel beaten in an alley, tossed out by the owners of the exclusive club after they'd found him stealing from the till. Clive had told her every secret he knew and Nestra had used the information to take control of the sexist club. Part of me admired what she had done, while another part considered her as corrupt as the men she reviled.

"Yes," I said aloud. "You are very kind. Noble, not just in birth, but in deed. I must ask. Have you heard anyone talking about bringing slaves through Hokku? Or taking emigrants before they go to space, fudging the books so no one realizes they've returned to Renga?"

She frowned, looked down at her hands, twisting the errant braid once again.

"Not me, of course. Slavery is not something I would ever get involved in," she began. I held my breath, stopped myself from snorting. Of course, Nestra wouldn't need slaves. She knew how to twist people to her side with money and manipulation. She had no need to bend them to her will the way a slaver would. Nestra didn't want to just be obeyed, she wanted to be adored.

"But I have heard talk. Some of my employees, some of them come from the streets. You understand. They've seen everything. There is a girl at one of my clubs, she escaped from the type of people you're talking about. Never told me much – frankly, I didn't want to know the details." Why would she, I wondered, imagining the possible business complications such knowledge could create. "But she might know something."

"She would?" I asked, excited. Could this really be a lead?

She shrugged, pouting a bit as she looked me over. "Not to you, though. The ears, you understand. She hates kems, I don't know why."

"Not even if you put in a good word for me?" I prodded.

"I can't. You understand. I wouldn't want to seem as if I was ordering her to talk to you." This time I was the one who frowned, not that she noticed. For a moment, I thought about throttling her with that braid. "Still, she's a sucker for cute guy. You have a friend you could bring? Someone who could do the talking for you?"

My violent daydream evaporated and I grinned. "I might," I said. Truth was, I knew just the person. "Do you think you could write down her name and where I can find her?" I held my notepad for her while she wrote down the information, then flipped back to the signatory page and watched her scrawl her name with a feminine flourish.

"Thank you so much," I gushed, putting away my things and kipping up to my feet. "I won't forget this, really. You've been a great help."

"Anytime," she said, sounding bored. "I don't suppose you can help me at all? Bring more of the feed?"

"Sorry, as you know, no one knows where to get more. The manufacturers seem to have disappeared for good." Disappeared, I thought, thanks to the Enso. No one would ever get their hands on Bartholomew Hill, the kitchen witch who'd been concocting the feed under duress, once Viv and Ava had taken him under the Enso's wing. He had resided with them for a while until they'd found him the perfect place to spend the rest of his days under an assumed name, fishing from his cabin beside a beautiful lake with mountain views. A new home, where no one would ever find him or force him to make the feed again. Even I had no idea where they'd hidden him away from seeking eyes.

I prayed the slavers hadn't been as good at hiding Henry.

CHAPTER 11

like birds, we preen – shine!
I'll be your wingman tonight
among feathers bright

I was running on empty. I'd delivered all my mail, and now I just wanted to crash for a few hours and load up on carbs. The couch at Jericha's flat had been calling my name for the last hour. I was finally in the home stretch, bounding along her hallway to pound on the door. My friend opened the door, looking annoyed, but when she saw my face her expression shifted to joy.

"Nikta, you're early!"

"I am?"

"Well, okay, you said you weren't sure what day you'd get back. I just assumed you'd be in Prime for a while." She grabbed me and hugged me hard, pulling my pack from me when she released me. "Not that I'm not glad to see you! Come in, take a load off. I was just about to eat."

I could smell it, something sweet and spicy. Jericha was a great cook. "Mmm, what are we having?"

"Pad thai. I picked up some fresh watermelon, too, I was going to juice it. You want?"

"Absolutely! Can I help?"

"No, just go wash up." She eyed the dirty boots I'd left at the door. My legs surely weren't much cleaner: I could feel the grit of the trail coating my face and arms. "Go on, take your time. I'll have everything ready by the time you come out."

Not one to argue with a free meal and shower, I made my way to the bathroom, taking care as I stripped down not to shake out any road dust onto the spotless floor. I turned on her shower and reveled in the feel of the water as it flowed unfettered along the slight curves of my body. Careful to keep the water out of my ears, I lathered up generously and washed everything – twice. The apartment boasted a bath, too, but it was small and I decided I would rather unwind chatting with Jericha than soaking in the cramped space. Still, I filled the nearby sink and quickly scrubbed my shirt and underthings, pulling out the drying rack recessed above the tub to hang them up. I chose my travel clothes based on their weight and packability, which meant thin fabrics that dried quickly. I knew everything would be ready to re-pack before I even fell asleep that night.

I rubbed some of Jericha's fancy face cream into my cheeks, fluffed up my hair and pulled on a fresh change of clothes. Back in the living room, Jericha was just laying out three large bowls of steaming noodles, bits of vegetables and peanuts poking up among the ribbons. A deep pink juice filled several oversized glasses and my mouth started to water. I loved being on the trail, really I did, but camp food couldn't compare with a meal like this.

"Napkins?" A deep voice rumbled from the kitchen.

"Yeah, chili sauce, too," Jericha called back.

A moment later her roommate, Reno Klein walked into the room brandishing both items. He smiled at me, looking nervous. "Nikta," he said, sitting down without quite meeting my eyes.

A month ago I'd saved him from the clutches of Otto Torriko, the manufacturer of the feed. Reno had been stealing from Jericha, taking little pieces of her qualitchka vine and selling it to Otto so they could make the magical drug. Her plant had almost died – worse, so had we. Jericha had found it in her heart to forgive Reno, keeping him on as a roommate despite his betrayal. I knew he hadn't really meant to hurt anyone, knew he just hadn't been thinking clearly under the influence of the drug, but still... He seemed to have given up his partying and womanizing since then. But how long would it last? I was glad it wasn't my apartment, glad I didn't have to decide whether to keep him or toss him. As it was, though, I had an idea of how he could start to repay me for saving him.

I smiled at him, hiding my teeth so he knew I meant no threat, and dug into my noodles. For a few minutes, the only sound in the room was the occasional slurp and gentle knocking of wooden chopsticks against heavy porcelain.

"So, what do you want to do tonight, Nikta? You're our guest, it's up to you. I have work in the morning but if you want to go out we can," Jericha offered.

"You know me, I'd rather stay in and catch up."

"My mother sent me a new mah-jongg set last week," Reno said. "You girls know how to play?"

"A bit," I said. "Unfortunately, I actually have somewhere I need to be. And I was hoping you'd come with me."

"Me?" Reno said, looking confused.

"And you," I told Jericha. "There's this club I want to check out, Champagne. Have you heard of it?"

Jericha choked on her juice. "The strip club?"

I swallowed. "Is that what it is? I didn't realize..."

"I'm not going to complain, but what makes you want to go there?" Reno asked. I sighed, realizing there was no way I could pass this off as a simple night of fun now. So I told them everything I knew about Henry and his family, about the slave rings on Hokku, and Nestra Laroche.

"Damn," Reno swore when I finished. "That's some heavy stuff. Sounds more dangerous than tangling with the feed."

"It could be," I admitted.

"So, you want us to what, chat up the girls at this club for you, find a lead?" Jericha asked.

"Not you. Him. We only need to talk to one girl, but Nestra says she won't talk to just anybody. She doesn't like kets, but she'll go soft for a handsome man."

Reno grinned, a bit of his former confidence bubbling to the surface. There was the womanizing hunk I'd met a month ago, I thought. And in that moment, I knew we had this.

"You think I'm handsome?" he said, preening.

Jericha smacked him in the shoulder. "You know you are, you ass."

"Yes. You are," I agreed. "And you owe me. So go get gussied up, make yourself as hunky as you can, and let's go meet Tulsi Flagg."

An hour later, I was seated at the bar, trying my best to ignore the young men and women gyrating on the five stages placed strategically around the room. Unfortunately, large mirrors along the walls made this nearly impossible. Besides, how could you not look? A young man, barely legal, was making obscene gestures as he slithered towards the audience and I found it almost as hard to look away as it was to watch. I'd never been in a strip club before, and I hoped I wouldn't ever have to return.

"Jericha, if you ever make me come here for a bachelorette party, I will make you regret it," I growled and she laughed, patting my shoulder.

"You'll survive," she said, and I wasn't sure if she meant tonight or the hypothetical hen night.

Reno had disappeared into the crowd when we'd arrived, distancing himself from us to chat with the wait-staff. I had to admit, he was smooth. I'd seen the way the waitresses practically melted under his attention. Flirting may have been their job, but Reno was a master.

Finally, he came back to us. His hair was mussed, his shirt was unbuttoned and rumpled, and he was grinning.

"I forgot how much fun this can be." He slid onto a barstool next to me and waved the bartender over, ordering a round of shots for the three of us.

"So, how'd it go?" I asked.

"Great. I got three girls numbers and a free lap dance," he confessed.

"Ew, she meant with Tulsi, you ape," Jericha said, rolling her eyes.

"I know what she meant," he laughed. "Your girl finishes her set in a minute. So drink up and get ready."

He pointed to the corner stage where a tasseled girl was shimmying, the glitter and sequins painted in lines along her naked skin glinting in the light, dazzling and hypnotizing her viewers.

"You want me to come with you? Won't that distract her from your fine charms?"

He barked with laughter. "Not possible. Don't worry about me. You just watch and make sure I ask the right questions."

"Okay," I said, shrugging.

"Great. Now, shots!" He passed out the small glasses and we slammed them back, the fiery clear liquid burning our throats.

"I'll stay here, thanks," Jericha gasped, taking a sip of the sweet honey wine she'd been drinking to chase away the fire.

"Suit yourself," Reno shrugged. "Back in five."

He slid off his seat and pulled me with him. Tulsi was just wrapping up her dance, taking a deep, bosom-dangling bow and allowing her admirers to thrust their money in her most private of places. As she disappeared backstage, Reno increased his pace.

"Hurry," he muttered. "These girls don't hang around long after their shift is up."

"She has to get dressed at least, doesn't she?" I asked, jogging to keep up with him.

Reno only snorted, which I took to be a no.

A couple of female bouncers stood by the entrance to the back, but Reno had already made friends with them and they only smiled broadly as he passed. "I'll be back in flash, Candy, Ginger," he promised. "Then maybe we can finish that dance," he said and they giggled.

Yuck.

"How do you do it?" I asked. Reno was hot, but I'd never felt any urge to fall for his charms.

"It's a gift," he said with a wink. "Come on, there she is."

In the back, I'd expected to find dressing rooms but there were only racks of costumes scattered through the bright open space, the music of the club dully pounding in the distance, lit mirrors lining the walls. Tulsi was knotting a plain brown wrap dress around her waist, the hem skimming the top of her calves. She'd already removed most of the crystals on her face and pulled her hair back into a severe bun. She looked like any other young woman coming off work – if you didn't notice the sequins peeking out from below her collar to skim along her chest or the shimmer on her legs. The latter, she set about hiding as she zipped on a pair of sleek knee-length boots.

She slipped out the back door just before we reached her.

Reno caught the door in his hand and followed, calling her name. I pulled my hood over my head and stayed behind in the shadows.

She paused, stiffening when she saw us. "Who's asking?"

Her accent was rough, off-world. I wondered idly where she'd come from, if coming here to strip in a night club had been everything she'd hoped for.

"A friend of Lady Laroche," Reno purred. He might not have been ket, but he knew how to use his voice in all the right ways. "Reno."

"Yeah? What do you want?" she asked with narrowed eyes.

"She told me you were her best dancer, and she was right. I'm starting up a club of my own cross-world, looking for only the best. Maybe you're interested?"

Her face lit up, then shuttered. "Can't. My son is getting treatment here. I can't go anywhere for another year, not until his lungs have cleared up."

"Ah. That's a shame. I've been having a hard time finding all the girls I need. Young men, too. Someone said I'd have better luck on Hokku, that that's the place to find hard workers, you know anything about that, doll?"

She should have ignored him, gone home, just as any girl would have brushed off another man. You could tell she wanted to. But Reno's hand rested on hers and his eyes gazed deeply into hers like she was the only girl in the world. For the first time, I was watching Reno in action and I had to wonder – what was it about him that made women drop to their knees? It had to be more than just his good looks. Whatever it was, Jericha and I seemed to be immune.

Against all odds, she took a step closer to him, so near her breasts brushed against his chest.

"The slavers?" she whispered. "You can't. They're not right. Their leader, the things they do. You don't want to get involved. Ask some of the other girls here, they'll go with you. I would."

"But they're not you. I need someone special. Maybe on Hokku-"

"I'm not special," she said bitterly. "When my son and I came through Hokku, they grabbed me and a couple kems, but they didn't want me. Tossed me back on a transport here, along with my boy, thank Yeshu. You don't need to go to Hokku, not if you really want to find them. I've met a guy, he does side-work for the slavers. He comes in here sometimes, I've heard him talking. That's who you should find."

"Okay," Reno said agreeably. "What's his name?"

"I'm not sure, I haven't seen him in a while. Something to do with cars. Rod, maybe? Not Tank..." She shook her head, frowning. "He's got real long hair, I'd know him if I saw him. Give me your number," she said eagerly. "I can call you next time he comes in."

Reno started to open his mouth but stopped when I stepped forward and put a hand on his shoulder.

"I don't think that will be necessary. Axel Lyell. Does that sound familiar?"

"Yes!" she said, beaming. She still grasped Reno's hand tightly. "Axel, that's it! I'm not sure about the last name though. You think it's him?"

"I do. Reno, we can go now."

"Can I still have your number?" she asked, tugging him closer.

"I'd love to... but you have a kid," Reno said carefully. "I'm not the guy you want."

"You are," she insisted.

He looked down at her, smoothed the hair from her face. Leaned down and kissed her forehead. Like a blessing.

"I'm not." Gently, he used his free hand to peel her fingers from his and stepped away. "Thank you, Tulsi."

Her eyes filled with tears as he stepped away and confusion etched her face, but she nodded.

"Come on," Reno said quietly to me, throwing an arm around my shoulders and leading me back inside.

"Reno, what the hell just happened?" I hissed. What I'd just seen, that wasn't normal. It was like he was a siren, a pheromone-laden honeypot. Except I sensed no pheromones, no magic, nothing out of the ordinary. "What are you?"

"Just a guy," he sighed, shoving his hands in his pockets.

"I think you're more than that," I insisted as we wound our way back through the dressing area. I watched the way the women stopped to ogle him, some of the men, too.

"You're wrong." He pointed his chin towards Jericha where she was nursing a pint at the bar. "Now, why don't you take our girl home. I've got an appointment to keep."

His voice was light, his words insisting he was the same party-boy I'd known, but I'd glimpsed the truth. Reno Klein was different. More than human, yet not ket, either. But what?

And did it matter? If Reno wanted to tell us who he was, what he was, he would. For now, he was only Reno – the man who'd just taken me one step closer to finding Henry. Ginger and Candy were already running their hands along his arms, claiming him like they'd won a toy at the fair. His eyes met mine, begging me to understand, to just let it go.

"Thank you, Reno."

"Anytime, Nikta." His shoulders sagged with relief. Then he let Ginger and Candy pull him behind some curtains into their sweet wonderland.

CHAPTER 12

rings of truth wade towards the shore
escaping the drowning stones

Jericha left early in the morning for work, tip-toeing out while I still slept. We'd stayed up late the night before, buffing our nails and trading news about friends and family. Reno hadn't come back and I didn't say anything to Jericha about what I'd noticed. Home, away from the throbbing lights and bare skin, the club had seemed like some sort of absurd dream. We'd drunk a lot, and I found myself questioning what I'd seen.

It was almost noon when I woke and I reveled in the limb-loosening decadence of sleeping in. On camping trips in the wilds, I'd been taught to sleep like a cat, always ready for danger. Even though post runners like me didn't have tight deadlines to adhere to, I'd always kept myself on a self-imposed schedule, my work ethic pushing me to run faster, do my best. I rarely slept in, even between runs.

Memories from the night before trickled in and I realized I had less right than usual to laze about. The Gunjabmi's were counting on me. Every day that went by, Henry could be getting further and further away from them, enduring Buddha knows what. I sprang to my feet and set about cleaning up, starting with putting away the comfy bed-roll Jericha had provided for the night. Once that was stowed, I cleaned my teeth and washed my face. I did a quick sniff test, confirmed my most recent shower was still in good effect, and pulled on my freshly laundered clothes. Some more of Jer's artisanal face moisturizer, a smear of lip balm and I was ready to get to work.

First stop: Precinct 8.

When I got there the front desk was being lorded over by an unfamiliar man. I politely asked to see Detective Pearce, but was rebuffed, told I'd have to make an appointment. The man sneered at me with disdain, staring at my slitted eyes as if he thought I was a dangerous cobra who would strike him the moment he looked away. The longer we locked eyes, the more tempted I was to do just that. Rather than flash my CCPD token the way I usually did, I thought I might just stay in this contest for a while. At least until I won.

Alas, it wasn't to be.

"Fee, you idiot. What in Buddha's balls do you think you're doing, keeping a CCPD operative from her work? Stop flirting with the lady and send her in," Bex Montana razzed the desk cop, slapping him on the back and hooting with laughter for good measure. "Sorry about that, ma'am. Kozan, was it?"

"Yes," I said, momentarily stymied again by her use of the word "ma'am." Had the creams not been helping? Just how old did I look, anyway?

"Never forget a face," she said with a wink, tapping her forehead.

"Me neither," I said, coming back to my senses and flashing her a grin. "Thanks, Officer Montana." I made sure to use her title, hoping to instill a little respect for the feminine mystique in her fellow cop, who watched our exchange with a slack jaw.

"Anytime. And call me Bex." She thrust out her hand and I gave it a good shake.

"Nikta."

"I remember. Go on in, Pearce is chest deep in reports right now, he's been at his desk all morning."

"Ohalo, Bex-san." I nodded politely at her and ducked through the doors into the belly of the beast, ignoring Bex's fellow gatekeeper entirely as I went.

I saw Jonah's dark head bent over his desk and looked away. He didn't want to be bothered, I reminded myself. I ducked into Lyric's office before Jonah could see me, but I couldn't help watching him through the frame.

"Can I help you, Kozan?" Lyric's voice held amusement and I realized I'd forgotten to knock.

"Detective!" I said, feeling silly. Honestly, my mother had taught me better than this. I bowed my head, begging forgiveness for the rude intrusion. "My apologies, I did not mean to just barge in."

"Not a problem. I was just looking over some cold cases that might relate to Gunjabmi's."

"Really?" I said, walking over to his desk to get a look at the papers spread before him.

"All confidential, of course," he said, shuttling them back into their folders and placing his hand over the named tabs.

I blushed. "Sorry. Again." I ducked my head and sank into one of the worn seats in front of his desk. Still, I couldn't help noting how thin the files were, and how high the stack of folders lifted his hand off the desk. So many missing people with meager trails to follow. Hopefully, I could change all that.

"I have some information I think might help."

"You do?" Surprise was evident in his voice, and something else.

"Yes. I dropped off a letter at Lady Laroche's yesterday and it occurred to me that with her connections, she might know something. She was happy to talk, hoping I might know where she could get more of the feed."

Pearce shook his head. "Still chasing the dragon, eh?"

"She misses the rainbows," I said, shrugging. "I made sure she knew it wouldn't be coming back on the market. She was very disappointed. Still, she was willing to tell me what she knew about the slavers."

"She's involved?" He asked, straightening as he pulled a notepad in front of him and started jotting down notes.

"No, no, nothing like that. But she runs some dance clubs, you know?"

"Nice word for them. Nestra's little clubs stop two steps short of prostitution, if you want my opinion."

"And after what I witnessed last night I would have to agree with you. But Nestra's money making schemes aren't my interest. Henry is."

"Okay, go on."

"Well, you know how things are at her places. Some of the people working for her are little more than kids. Street kids, to be exact. Nestra's heard things."

"Funny, I can't recall her ever reporting anything here," he drawled.

"No, she wouldn't. She's a businesswoman, and she minds her own. Anyway, she told me about this girl at her club, Champagne."

"I know it." He scribbled the name down, staring hard at the paper. "Don't look at me like that. It's my business to know these sorts of places."

"How do you know how I was looking at you?"

"I could feel the lasers burning a hole in my skull. The girl? She have a name?"

"Tulsi. Tulsi Flagg." I watched him write it down. "You don't need to talk to her though. I've already done it."

"What?" His green eyes flashed angrily. "You went there? Do you know how dangerous that was? The people who go to those places-"

"Relax, I brought backup. Nestra told me Tulsi had a thing against kets, told me to bring a pretty face so I brought my friend and her roommate." I decided it would be best to keep Reno's name out of Lyric's little book.

"More civilians? What were you thinking?"

"I dunno," I said, flicking my ears back. "Maybe that someone who really cares should be involved?"

"That's not fair. I took the case when your brother wouldn't. You think I'd be in this job if I didn't care? The benefits aren't that great, trust me."

He was right, I thought, feeling slightly guilty. I hated it when people judged me for what I looked like, and here I was, judging him by his peers.

"Sorry," I said. "The guy you brought, tell me he at least knows how to fight."

"Reno?" I snorted. "Hardly. But I can take care of myself, remember?"

"Yeah, until you can't," he reminded me. "Reno, huh. The same guy who was selling Torriko qualitchka for the feed?"

I nodded, feeling bad I'd let the name slip.

"So, you decided you'd rather trust a criminal and ex-addict to run recon with you than me?" Now, Lyric looked more hurt than angry.

"This from the guy who thought I tried to blow him up a month ago?" I reminded him. "Please. Reno is hot and the ladies like him. He's reformed, mostly, and he wanted to help. End of story. Besides, I hardly think your wife would appreciate you going out to chat up young strippers."

"My wife?" A shadow passed over his face. "I'm not married."

"But your ring-"

"A memento from another life," he said, cutting me off. "Next time, try not to think so much for yourself and consider what your brother would want you to do."

"Jonah!"

"Yeah, Jonah. He may be a pain in your ass but at least he understands procedure and knows how to follow the rules. Rules we've put in place to protect not just ourselves, but you, too, dammit."

"Fine. Whatever." I stood, starting to sling my pack over my shoulder.

"Aren't you going to tell me what Flagg told you?"

"Shit. Right." I sunk back into my seat, cradling my pack in my lap as I slouched down. "She didn't know much. Said she and some kems were grabbed by thugs on Hokku when she immigrated here, but they changed their minds and didn't keep her. She was pretty scared to talk about it, but Reno was able to sweet talk her. She told us there was a guy who comes into the club sometimes that does side-work for the slavers, she's heard him talking."

"Did you get a name?"

"I did. Axel."

Pearce whistled. "Lyell?"

"How many Axels can there be?" I asked.

"Not many, when you factor in the scumbag part."

"Exactly." I watched him make some more notations in his book. "So? What are we going to do?"

"We? Nothing. You are going to go about your business, tell your friends I'm on the case, and let me do my damn job."

"But-"

"But nothing, Nikta. Did you hear yourself? They took kems. Not Tulsi. Just kems. You can't go traipsing around asking questions anymore, it's too dangerous."

I snorted. "First of all, I don't traipse. Second, Henry isn't a kem."

Lyric shrugged. "Still. You keep your nose out of this from now on, you hear."

"Whatever you say," I said, shrugging. "Can I go now?"

The detective looked at me, his face unreadable as he searched mine. Two could play that game. We squared off for a few more seconds.

"Fine, go," he finally said.

"Ohalo, Detective," I said easily. I was almost out the door when I heard him sigh.

"Ohalo, Kozan. Just remember what I said. Curiosity isn't healthy for cats."

I bristled. "I'll do that, Detective." I pulled a wake of air with me as I left the room. I heard his papers scatter, swears filling the vacuum I'd created, and the door slammed shut on the breeze.

CHAPTER 13

two birds fly as one
then separate, howling wind
storm clouds gather - dark

Jonah glanced up, like many of the other cops in the room. Most went back to their work, some gave me hard looks. Jonah waved. Surprised, I smiled back and walked over to his desk.

"Ohalo, brother. How are you?"

"I'm good," he said, looking up at me with happy eyes. I hadn't seen him this relaxed and glad to see me in years. What had changed? My ears twitched, picking up snippets of conversation about us, but tried to keep them facing forward towards Jonah. My nostrils flared and I realized Jonah smelled different. A floral soap was layered under his aftershave. Ah. He'd spent the night with a woman. Joyce?

"Wanna grab lunch?"

"Huh?" I started.

"Lunch, Nikta. Want to grab some? I know it's a little early but-"

"Lunch would be great."

"Good. I just finished a report and I'm supposed to be working a case all afternoon. If I don't head out now, I might not eat until the end of the day. Let's go, before anything else comes up."

"Okay," I said, feeling game. I hadn't seen this side of Jonah since before the Olympic scouts came to Prime, since the last time we'd played hooky together, skipping school to hang with some of his friends. I liked it.

He slipped on a light jacket and we walked outside, waving to the Bex as we passed.

"I like her," I said as we hit the sidewalk.

"Who, Montana?"

"Bex? Yeah. She's nice. Way more personable than most of the other guys who man that desk."

"Yeah. She's a good kid."

"She's almost the same age as us."

"Yeah. Still a noob, though."

I rolled my eyes, wondering if the slight woman would always be a "kid" to the guys at the precinct. I let it slide though, not wanting to ruin the good vibe we had going between us.

We didn't have far to go, just a few doors down the block before we came to a dumpling house. Jonah pushed open the door and held if for me as I entered. The smells were divine. The shop was run deli-style, with sticky rice cakes, fluffy stuffed buns and at least twenty different styles of dumplings gracing the display cases. The line at the counter was ten people deep, despite the earliness of the hour. We waited quietly in line and then placed our orders: Wild boar buns, delicate shrimp shumai, and a small salted fish cake for Jonah; a sweet plum rice cake and spicy curried dumplings in a coconut broth for me. Efficiently plated in simple wooden bowls, the server handed us two metal trays and we took our bounty to a corner table by the window.

Again, I couldn't help notice how different Jonah seemed, how much more comfortable in his own skin he was. Normally, I would have expected him to seat us as far out of the way as possible, where no one would see us. Who was I kidding? A month ago he would never have brought me to a place so close to the precinct. Nowhere we might have been seen by his peers.

"This is nice. Great food," I said, tasting the soup. "You come here a lot?"

"Most days. There's a little Mexican joint around the corner I like to hit up, and a great pizza place that specializes in the old-style. Joyce thinks I should be more practical, bring my own meals to work like she does, save some money."

"She's probably right. But these dumplings!"

"I know," he agreed, closing his eyes as he bit into his own pork bun, the white fluffy dough around it still steaming. "How can she expect me to make do on cold wraps?"

"It'd be a crime," I said, and he laughed.

"Absolutely." He took a sip of his water. Stared at his plate. "She wants us to get an apartment together."

"Big step," I said, cocking my head to one side. "How do you feel about that?"

"Not sure." He shrugged and met my eyes. "Like you said, it's a big step. I haven't lived with a woman since... well, since you and Ma."

"Living with Joyce would be different, obviously," I said, trying to stay neutral. My mind was starting to run with the idea, imagining Jonah in a one-God house. No altar for the ancestors. No festival days. Would they get married? Have babies? What if they had a child with magic, ears or slitted eyes? Would Joyce be able to love a child like that? More importantly, would a child like that be able to love itself with her as a mother?

I didn't know any of the answers to my questions, and I tried to stop them from coming as I watched Jonah form his next words.

"She liked you, you know," he said, surprising me. "She's not as bad as you think she is."

"I never said-"

"You didn't have to."

"Okay, fine. You know me, and I know you. How serious are you about this woman, Jonah? Because I worry about what will happen if you guys stay together – could she really love your children, even if they come out like me, or Viv, or Ava?"

"Of course!"

"If you believe that, then I wish you all the best. She obviously makes you very happy – you're glowing. Maybe you should go for it. Move in with her. You both work a dangerous job. You don't know what tomorrow might bring. Grab as much happiness as you can, while you can."

"Like you? I don't see you getting serious with anybody, haven't since...well, since forever."

"Only because getting serious isn't what makes me happy," I joked, sticking my tongue out at him and refusing to think of Kuma or Innis. "There are so many beautiful birds in the sky, who am I to listen to only one song? Besides, you know me, I'm a nomad. The only roots I seek are our own." I reached out and grasped his hand. "I've missed you, brother."

"I've missed you, too." He gave my fingers a squeeze and we went back to eating. Jonah, as when we were kids, finished before me. He leaned back in his chair and watched me eat.

"So tell me, how is the great detective today? What's he got you working on now?"

He tried to keep his voice light, but I could tell it still bothered him that Lyric had roped me into contracting with their department.

"Nothing, I was just checking in."

"Did he turn up any leads about that kid you were worried about?"

"No. I dug up some information on someone who might be connected to slavers, but nothing concrete. Lyric wants me to stay out of it now."

"Probably wise," he said. And he was probably right, but it still rankled. I decided to change the subject.

"Anyway, I was out on Hot Creek a few days ago, delivering mail. Did you know some religious freaks have claimed the land near Aligna's Well?"

"Really? Makes sense, I guess, I mean it's supposed to be holy and all." Jonah had never been much for the gods, old or new.

I stabbed the last bite of gooey, sweet rice from my plate and savored the fruit on my tongue. "It *is* holy. And they're not just hanging out there, they've built a wall around the place. They're charging for entry, can you believe it?"

Jonah tugged on his ear, thinking. "Good way to make money, I guess."

"But, it's public land. It's always been public, open and free to anyone."

Jonah shrugged. "Under the Homesteading Act they can claim whatever land they want.

"Not public waterways," I argued.

"True. But the pool isn't really a waterway, and the land is theirs."

I growled, frustrated. "It's a holy place. Sacred. They're making pilgrims pay ten yendar to cross their land, another thirty to swim. And they're barring kems entirely."

"Huh. Well, that's not nice. But I'm not sure it's illegal, either."

"Of course it's illegal. It's discriminatory!"

"But it's their land. I'm not sure if-"

"Oh my gods. You really are starting to think you're one of them. Wake up, Jonah. You're a ket, too. What happens when you and Joyce have a baby and it looks more like our side of the family? Will you care about our rights then?"

Jonah's face had gone pale. "That's not fair. I'm a cop, Nikta, I have to look at things from both sides. From the law's side."

"If the law says it's okay for off-worlders to come and steal our most holy lands, then the law can go screw itself."

"Nikta-"

"No seriously, brother. I'm sorry if this ruffles your feathers, but I can't just be a good little ket and not speak up when I see bad shit going down. And those people, The Seekers? They're not just racist – they're creepy. Like a cult."

Jonah sighed. "I'll do what I can, look into the land laws. Run a check on the group. But I doubt I'll be able to do much. Religious groups are protected by the Freedom of Religion, Bodies and Beliefs Act."

I made a face and a strong breeze circled the table, ruffling Jonah's hair.

"I don't write the laws, you know."

"I know," I said, calming. "I'm sorry. I shouldn't have gotten mad at you. I just hate to see the land being treated like that. Boxed up, as if any one person has a right to own it. And I worry about you."

"More than you should. I've been taking care of myself a long time now. I'm happy."

"I know, I can see that you are. I'm glad. Truce?" I wasn't really glad about anything, but I didn't want to leave things on a bad note between us.

"Truce." He shook my hand and stood. "I should be heading back now. What about you?"

"Yeah. Things to do, people to see." I shrugged, forcing a brightness I didn't feel.

"You heading back to Prime?"

I shook my head, pulling my pack over my shoulder. I smiled at him, ignoring the uneasy knot of concern that had settled into my chest. "Not yet. Tomorrow, probably."

"Okay. Well, maybe I'll see you before you leave. If not, next time?"

"For sure. Ohalo, Jonah."

"Ohalo, sister." We embraced, a brief show of familiarity, and then we went our separate ways.

CHAPTER 14

return to the flock, gather!
beware the two-faced shepherd

The large, ornate door of the Enso stood before me in an impressive display of gold, copper, silver, and calressium.

The Enso of Chalinex City was considered the most powerful on Renga, and it had an entrance to match. Interstellar imagery mingled with windswept flowers, dancing flames and rivers of calressium tinged blue. The artwork was gorgeous, but all for show. As an embassy of magic and a prime target for kem-haters, the entire embassy was shielded with magic – the door most of all.

Designed to keep regs out, only a natural-born magic user held the keys to open the door from the outside. I knew the protocol. If I'd been a reg, I would have had to knock – and admittance would only be granted if I'd already taken the time to make an appointment. Me? All I had to do was show the door I was worthy.

The door hummed like a busy hive of clockwork bees, waiting. Feeling feisty, I conjured my dragon, letting it play and circle my body one, two, three times before sending it through the sculptured landscape of the door, letting it run among the flowers for a moment and then watching it dive into the river, the blue light rippling through the metal like a splash. The hive hummed more loudly, conferring amongst itself, and then the door began to shimmer with a blinding light, the gears turned, and the door walked itself off its hinges to reveal the inner sanctum of the Enso.

I heard a giggle behind me and saw two children hiding near the steps, watching. I winked at them, called my dragon back and watched it splinter into a riot of butterflies to fly above the children's heads. They clapped gleefully, watching the show, and I stepped inside knowing the display would end in a few moments but their experience would last a lifetime.

Once I was indoors, the door scuttled back into place, its gears clicking and murmuring to themselves as it resumed its watch. The Enso's arachnid automaton click-clacked towards me down the dim hallway, waited patiently as I slipped off my boots.

"I'm here to see Viv and Ava."

The spelled machine dipped its head, snapping its two front legs together to create a brilliant orb hovering above it, and then scurried down the hall. I followed, knowing it would lead me to the twins. The spider stopped before a pair of golden gates set with gears, made a few gestures and claps with its front legs and moved back towards me. There was an instant response, the hum of gears unmistakable as the entrance folded in on itself neatly, pressing against the walls on either side of the archway to create an intricate design, levers and gears now resembling a bronzed bower.

The office was formally appointed, impressively built by magic with three seamless walls and a dome above that allowed in an abundance of starlight. The space had been designed to stun regs, make them appreciate the favor our kind did for them by policing its own. What most did not realize was that the spaces were also designed to balance our magic, to allow us to harness the elements more easily. It was this sort of attention to detail that made the Enso a force to be reckoned with, its agents the most powerful mages on the planet.

Viv and Ava were seated at the huge central table, going over paperwork.

"Hey cuz, what's shaking?" Viv said, leaning back in her seat with a grin on her face, her short hair slick and wet, combed back from her face.

Ava looked up from a file, her eyes slow to focus, blinking slowly. Her pale locks cascaded like sheets of ice over her shoulders. "Ohalo, Nikta. Nice to see you."

"Ohalo, cousins." I gave them each a kiss on the cheek and settled into a nearby chair. "There are some things going on I think the Enso needs to know about."

"An official visit, then," Viv said, looking intrigued. "And here I thought you just missed us."

I laughed. "Miss you? I can't seem to stay away long enough for that. Listen, there's a new group settled near Aligna's Well-"

"The Night Seekers?" Ava interrupted me. "We've heard of them. Aligna's Well, that's in Prime's jurisdiction, though."

"I know. I'm not sure they're equipped to deal with this lot, though."

"Deal with them?" Viv asked. "What have they done? I thought they kept pretty much to themselves."

"They did. Lately though... The last time I went there to deliver mail, they refused to let me into the compound. My packages are always carry-with-care, requiring a signature. I had to leave without delivering the mail, a first for me."

"Okay, that's pretty shady. Thanks for letting us know."

"No, Viv, you don't understand. That's more of a PGPS issue, for sure. The real problem is that they've claimed the well. They're charging admission, and since no kems are allowed on the compound, ket pilgrims are going to be barred from the holy waters now. Hundreds of our own people each year, surely."

"They can't do that," Ava said, consternation setting her eyes aglow.

"That's what I told them. They didn't agree."

Ava and Viv looked at each other, communicating silently. Viv frowned and Ava didn't look pleased when she spoke, either.

"It's a land-use issue, unfortunately. You'll have to take it up with the police," Ava said.

"I did. CCPD says to let it go. I'll talk to the officials in Prime, of course, but I think they'll say the same."

Viv played with a white-hot ball of fire in her hand, turning it over, considering. "It's sickening, I know. But the only way to deal with issues like this is to get the laws changed – protect our holy spaces and more delicate ecosystems, get them registered as heritage sites, that sort of thing. It's something Ava and I have been working on for the past year, actually."

"Oh, that's great. How's it going?"

"Slow," Viv grumbled.

"We'll get there," Ava assured us, patting her sister on the shoulder. "These things take time."

"And Aligna's Well?"

"The Seekers will have no rights to that land, if the law gets written the way we want. Still, I think we should report the group's anti-ket sentiments to the Prime chapter, don't you, Viv?"

"Absolutely. I'll draft a letter now." The ball of fire winked out and she picked up a pen and paper.

"There, see? It'll all get sorted." Ava smiled at me. "Now, how about a cup of tea?" She stroked the spider who'd been sitting inert by her feet and it hopped onto all eight points and skittered off towards the kitchens.

"Tea is always appreciated, thank you. I do have another thing on my mind, though."

Viv paused in her writing to glance up at me, squinting one eye at me in mock scrutiny. "Uh oh. Here comes trouble," she joked.

"You know me too well," I said, winking. "But seriously, if you can help me on this one I'll consider it a personal favor."

"Ooh, sounds juicy!" Viv said, laying down the pen. "Spill."

I told them all about the Gunjabmi family, about Henry's strange letter, and what I'd found out from Lyric and Tulsi.

"You don't trust the cops to handle this on their own?" Ava asked, looking concerned as she passed me a steaming cup of jasmine tea. The spider had already returned, scorpion servers in tow with cakes, tea, cups and plates.

"Would you?" I asked

Ava opened her mouth, then closed it. "No, I suppose not. Not if it were you or Viv missing, no. But then, this boy, Henry? He's not family. Why do you care so much?"

"I don't know. I've asked myself the same question. I guess it's more about the people he's left behind, you know? I know what it feels like to be left behind. Family matters. The Gunjabmis can't do this on their own."

A look passed between them and Ava nodded at Viv, who spoke. "Okay. What can we do to help?"

"Anyone down for a field trip?"

Viv grinned, chomping down on a dainty tea cake. "I'm in."

An hour later Viv and I were at Axel's door. Ava had stayed behind to wrap up some work, saying she trusted us to handle things on our own. His apartment was an insane experiment in pomp and modernity, a shimmer of rainbows and mirrors. You couldn't see the wealthy residents within, but the building was designed to let you know they were there. The doorman took one look at Viv's badge marking her as an ambassador of the Enso and let us in immediately, showing us the way to the elevator.

I'd met the young woman manning the cubicle the last time I'd been here, a gum-snapping reg by the name of Zeddie.

"I remember you," she said enthusiastically as the doors slid closed and she punched in Axel's floor number. "PGPS, right?"

"Yes," I said, impressed. "Good memory. You still thinking of applying?"

"Filled out an application last week," she said with a grin.

"Good for you!" I said and meant it. "I can put in a good word for you at HQ. You looking to stay stationed here?"

"Never been anywhere else," she said, blowing a bubble and shrugging. The elevator had risen several floors above the streets, climbing the skin of the building like a tick and giving us a sprawling view of the city. "What's it like out there?"

"Big. Wild."

"Sounds epic."

"It is," I said, smiling. "You're gonna love it."

The elevator bell rang, signaling our arrival, and Viv and I stepped out into an opulent hall lined with an abundance of glass, brass and golden carpet. We padded down the hall to the fourth doorway of hammered brass, the lanterns flanking it flickering dimly in the starlight. I knocked and we waited.

"I had no idea you were such a good Samaritan," Viv broke her silence, keeping her eyes on the door.

"Yeah, right, I'm an angel in cat's clothing," I laughed.

Viv snickered.

The door swung open. I'd expected a servant or boy-toy, as usual, but this time Lyell himself opened the door, his long hair scraggled and oily.

"Ladies," he drawled, his eyes roving over our bodies. "To what do I owe the pleasure?"

"Try not to be such a sleaze, Lyell," Viv growled, brushing past him. She trailed a hand along the couch, turned and sat in a large arm-chair for all the world as if she were his queen. "Sit," she commanded, gesturing towards the sofa. And he did. Unable to help myself, I smirked as I prowled the room.

"Have I done something to step on the Enso's toes?" he asked sounding nervous now.

"I don't know, Axel, have you?" she said with a moue.

"No, of course not." His eyes darted to mine. "Look, I haven't seen nor heard from Torriko in weeks. I have no idea where the bastard is hiding out."

"Old news," my cousin purred, waving her hand dismissively. "We're not here for that."

Axel's shoulders slumped in relief and he fell back against the couch, folding his arms over his chest. "Well then, why are you here?"

Viv stared him down, toying with him like a cat with a mouse. Finally, she relented, looking at me. "Go on, tell the man."

I understood what she was doing. She'd come with me for backup: she'd primed the pump, and now it was my job to get the water flowing. With the Enso behind me, he'd be hard-pressed to refuse any request.

"We're looking for some people you know. People you work for."

His eyes narrowed. "Who?"

"Some folks we heard might be dabbling in the slave trade." Viv said quietly, almost sweetly. As she spoke, she toyed with a small flame in one hand.

Axel paled, eyeing the flame uneasily. "I don't have anything to do with that."

"Perhaps. Perhaps not. Honestly? You aren't our concern at the moment."

"If I say anything, I'm dead," he whispered, seemingly mesmerized by the growing ball of fire in her hand.

"There are many ways to die," she purred.

He swallowed.

"Give us a name, a location and we'll go," I said.

He laughed, a dark, dirty sound.

"Oh, they'd love to meet you. You're just their type."

"Yeah, we've heard they like kems," I hissed. "Doesn't explain why they've started taking reg boys from the Mudlands, though."

Axel looked surprised. "They wouldn't."

"You know any other slavers in the city?" I demanded.

"No, no one else. Only one person dares trade bodies through Hokku. I don't know no one who'd cross them, neither."

"Well, now you do." Viv said, tossing her flame at a candle and watching it catch and flare towards the ceiling before simmering down. The blood drained from Axel's face.

"Fine, fine, I'll tell you everything I know. Just, please, don't tell them how you found out. I'm not kidding when I say they'll kill me."

"Don't worry, Lyell, your secret is safe with us," Viv said sweetly. "Consider it another favor you'll owe us."

"Another?"

"Yes, we spared you once already for your work with Torriko. Three strikes, Axel. That's all you get. Maybe it's time you consider leaving the city for a spell."

He gulped. "Understood. I'm not stupid."

"Could have fooled me," I muttered. "Now, start talking."

"Right, yeah. I don't sell nobody, see. Sometimes, when these kids age out of the work, I help find them permanent positions, that's all."

"House slaves?" I asked, scowling.

"No, no, they get salaries, they can go anytime. By then though, they don't believe anyone else would want them. When you've been in that sort of trade, you don't feel fit for regular society no more, you know? People like me, I find them a place where they'll fit."

"You're a real humanitarian, Axel," I said.

"Hey, I do what I can. I know what it's like to have limited options." He looked at us pointedly, hugging himself tightly and I wondered. What had he endured to get where he was today? Unbidden, an ember of sympathy kindled in my heart and I tried to tamp it down.

"Go to Lilac Street, check out The Blossoming Spa. You'll get all your answers there."

"The Blossoming?" Viv asked, surprised. "But, that's a legit business."

"Is it?" Axel raised an eyebrow. "Talk to the manager, Annalee, my date from the gala. She knows everything."

"You brought a ket slaver into my Circle?" Viv's jumped to her feet, flames snaking along both her arms, her hands balled into fists. "I ought to dust you right now."

"I didn't have a choice!" He cowered, shrinking into the sofa cushions as if they could save him.

I placed a hand on Viv's shoulder, knowing her fire wasn't for me. "Come on, he's not worth it. We've got what we need."

Viv bared her teeth, feral. "You have till moonrise to get out of town, Lyell. Or else we'll see just how flammable a reg can be."

"You wouldn't," he squeaked from behind a pillow.

"Try me," she said with dead heat.

"I'll go. Please, I'll go. Leave and I promise, I'll pack a bag right now."

"Viv," I said gently. "Come on."

All the candles in the apartment flared to life and one of the glass hurricane lamps nearby shattered from the sudden flare of heat. Axel whimpered but the flames on Viv's arms had subsided to a bare glimmer.

"Moonrise," she hissed one last time and swept from the room.

Axel peaked at me from behind the cushion he hugged to his chest and I tried not to giggle at the ridiculousness of it.

"I hope, for your sake, you haven't lied today."

"I swear, I haven't," he wheezed. I nodded, accepting his words. I followed Viv out the door, pausing to look back at him one last time.

"Ohalo, Axel Lyell. You survived the fire today. The circle surrounds you now – make your next choices wisely."

CHAPTER 15

white eye gazes down
people scurry, hurry home
lives change, stay the same

The elevator waited, Zeddie smiling, but Viv was nowhere in the hall. I waved to Zeddie and indicated I'd be taking the stairs. No way did I want to leave Viv on her own and I could only assume she'd decided to walk off some of her steam. I finally caught up with her in the street, lips drawn tight, foot tapping impatiently.

"Blossoming?" I asked.

"No. I promised the Arch-mage I'd do something for him today. Promise me you'll wait? We'll take care of everything tomorrow, I swear – but I need you to wait for me. Deal?"

I hesitated, saw sparks start to fly off of her. "Yes," I acquiesced reluctantly. "I'll wait. One day. That's all."

"Okay." She looked relieved. Keyed up, but no longer worried. I realized that as outraged as she was about the slavers, her concern had been reserved for one person: me. "You can hang out at the Enso tonight, of course. You coming?"

"I don't know, I thought I'd probably stay with Jericha. Plus, I have to check in at the office first. I hate to leave you, though. You sure you're okay?"

"Yeah, I'll be fine. I shouldn't have let him get to me like that. Ava always says-"

"Ava wasn't here. I think you did great. Just, don't blow anything up on the way home, okay? Yuki's watching, after all," I said, pointing at the white orb in the sky.

She laughed. "I'll try my best. See you, cousin."

She hugged me briefly and then took off at brisk pace towards the Enso. I looked at the sky, gauging my position, and then headed down another street towards the city's PGPS headquarters.

The sentries here still weren't used to me so it took a little longer to clear security. Once I'd passed through, I headed straight to the Postmaster's office. Vincent Sun was small and tough, like me. The ket's green eyes were so dark they almost appeared black, a startling contrast to his pale skin and soft gray hair. I knew it would be a mistake to ever underestimate this man.

I knocked on his door and watched his ears flick backward in displeasure, one ear notched from a sword fight with some bandits, if I was to believe the gossip. "What is it?"

Having just watched one ket almost go nuclear in a small, confined space, I was pretty sure I could handle Sun.

"Ohalo, Sun-sama." I ducked my head in a shallow bow.

"Do I know you?"

"Nikta Kozan, sir."

"Ah, yes, the carrier from Puraimura. Well, what do you want? Come here, I won't bite," he said wryly. "Sit down, my neck is killing me."

I approached and took a seat across from him at his desk. "I met a girl here in the city last month, a real go-getter. I suggested she apply for a job, and she didn't waste any time. Got in an application right away. I wanted to submit a recommendation, if you'll accept one."

"She impressed you that much?"

"She did, sir."

"What's so special about her?" His eyes narrowed. "You related?"

"No, sir."

"Then what? What's her story?"

"Honestly? I don't even know. She just seems like a good kid. She's eager, wants to see the world. And she's respectful."

"A ket?"

144

"No, which is part of what made her stand out, if I'm honest. She's a reg, but she doesn't have a drop of prejudice in her. Something I can't say for most of the regs I've met here in the city, if you don't mind me saying so."

"No, no. it's the gods-damned truth, we all know it. Chalinex is a cess-pool, don't know why I stay some days." He eyed me up and down, assessing me, deciding if he thought I was worth listening to. Apparently, I was, because a moment later he was puffing out his cheeks and had picked up a pen. "She wants to be a runner, like you?"

"I'm not sure that's the best position for her, she's never been out of the city. I was thinking she might be good for a transport team?"

"Driving one of the mail trucks to other towns? That's a possibility. No special skills needed there and we always send the drivers out in teams. Alright. What's her name?"

"Zeddie."

"Zeddie what?"

I smacked my forehead. "I forgot to ask. I can go back-"

"Nevermind, I'll figure it out. A reg named Zeddie, how many of them can there be? We don't get that many applications this time of year. Joanie will know. Damned woman thinks she knows everything, and she's usually right," he muttered to himself.

I chuckled and he looked up, frowning. "You still here? You got more to add?"

"No, I suppose that's it," I said, springing to my feet and backing towards the door. "Thank you, Sun-sama."

"You don't owe me anything. But if this girl turns out to be trouble, you'll hear it from me. PGPS is like a family, and I don't take kindly to people messing with my family, you hear?"

"I feel the same way, sir. Thank you, sir. "

He didn't answer, just nodded and looked back down at his desk, chewing on the end of his pen. I'd only taken a few steps away before he bellowed. "Joanie!"

A tall, willowy woman rose from one of the desks, squared her shoulders and slowly sauntered past me, rolling her eyes. Behind me, I heard her murmur something to Vincent, and then they started bickering good-naturedly back and forth. *Yeah, Zeddie will fit in just fine here*, I thought.

I made my way back to the sorting room and found the Master Sorter for the carry-with-care program. Boone, a terse woman whom I had yet to make smile, handed me full load: several things destined for Prime, a few local deliveries and some headed to the wilds. I complimented her earrings, which earned a gruff thanks, and left quickly. The place could certainly use a girl like Zeddie, someone with an easy smile might even shift the general atmosphere a notch towards friendly. At least Vincent dealt straight, no beating around the bush, no games.

I set about dropping off the local deliveries right away.

A tidy package for a woman from her beau who was building their dream home halfway across the planet: she said it contained gems he'd mined on their land, which she would then set herself in silver and gold and sell for a pretty penny at the weekend market. In another month or two, the house would be done and she'd join him. Of course, I asked to see her wares and wound up purchasing a pretty gold ring with shimmering green hiddenite shards and a perfectly round star sapphire. It fit my pinky just right.

A sheaf of business contracts for the president of Chalinex Investments, the biggest bank on the planet. He stayed on the phone the whole time, shouting angrily and avoiding eye contact with me while he signed for the delivery. For the millionth time, I voiced a silent thanks to the gods that they had steered me away from office work.

Rare, medicinal herbs for the shamanic healer working with Jericha's favorite acupuncturist. She'd pointed out the small healing center to me the week before, but I hadn't realized it harbored such a diverse cast of healers. Maybe the next time I was in town I'd book an appointment. I had a feeling I could use a few good soul retrievals. Gods knew I'd had a hole in my heart ever since Mama had died.

Even after I'd delivered all my local goods and trekked through a good portion of the city streets, I still felt restless. The streets were crowded since a lot of people had the day off. Half the restaurants were closed, and many of the banks and doctor's had shut early. People walked, enjoying the free time, basking in the starshine, smiling under the blended auspices of Yuki and Hokku. My legs burned for a run, but there was barely room to squeeze among the crowds. I felt hot. Stifled. How could they stand it? I wasn't used to being around so many people all the time. Compared to Chalinex, Prime was a ghost town.

Someone's shoulder bumped mine, hard, and I hissed in pain.

"Bakemato," I heard the man sneer as he walked the other way.

Normally, I would have said something, called him out on his racial slur, but in seconds he'd faded from view, absorbed by the crowd. I had a tough skin, words like his never hurt me.

Yet there I stood, clutching the straps of my bag near my shoulders, straining to catch my breath. I shook my head, turning, and almost collided with a woman my age.

"Watch it, yokai," she said angrily, stepping around me. The young child holding her hand gazed up at me curiously and she dragged him away, yanking him when he didn't keep up.

Tears sprang in my eyes, but I refused to give in. Refused to raise my hood, would not cover my ears. I wasn't going to hide, not for anyone. The boy was watching, and I wanted him to know I was a person.

Wanted him to know I was good. Not a demon, no matter what his mother might say. So I smiled at him, winked, and sent a small ghost of a butterfly to follow him, a glimmer of aquamarine light that only he and I noticed. He smiled, reaching out his hand, gaining another yank from his mother. He glared at her in consternation, then turned back to me. Caught at the butterfly, which burst into sparkling fragments. Waved at me, and was gone, consumed by the crush of people.

Tears ran down my cheeks, but I smiled, knowing one heart remained open. One heart would remember and grow, I hoped, to be kind.

CHAPTER 16

*play like the young, hitting hard
looking pretty, drawing blood*

Following the path of least resistance, I moved into empty spaces, sought avenues and alleyways with fewer people, fewer regs, less of everything. The streets began to clear, the buildings declining in age and quality, windows cracking, pavement turning to potholes and puddles.

I found myself in the Mudlands. A place where there was nothing to celebrate, no day off to enjoy. The poor didn't get days off, unless they had no work at all. The people here worked themselves to the bone and then collapsed in tired heaps. It was a neighborhood where a week's wages barely fed one person for a day. A sector of the city where drugs flowed like wine, dulling the hunger, dulling the pain of living in a city that didn't want them.

Didn't want me.

I skirted limbs that lay akimbo on the sidewalk, not daring disturb sleeping junkies. Assuming they slept. The reek of alcohol, sewage, and unwashed bodies overpowered my senses, but underneath it all ran the unease of decay, the rotten scent of the dead and diseased. Wrinkling my nose, I pondered my next steps. If I kept walking, eventually I would come to the edges of the Mudlands, either re-entering the prettier sectors of the city, or leaving it behind entirely. I wasn't sure which way I wanted to turn. Since I was here, a visit to the Gunjabmis might be warranted.

Except I wasn't sure I should add to their worries, not yet.

And so I walked, trying to center myself, trying to unearth my next direction. Few walked the deserted streets, although I did occasionally see youths here or there. They kept their heads down, avoiding trouble, walking quickly. Eventually, I realized they were all heading in the same direction and I decided to follow a rag-tag group of boys and girls who'd emerged into the street a block ahead.

Laughing quietly, pushing each other as they walked, the trio ducked into an abandoned warehouse, the majority of its windows miraculously intact and lit from within. I paused outside, looking up at the entrance. Spray-painted on the bricks, someone had inked a scene of the wilds – imagined, unreal, with leaves and trees I'd never seen. Animals peaked out from among the fronds, and words glimmered in glow-paint: Wild Things. The name wrestled a half smile from me. Was this a gang? An all-ages club? What was going on here?

Another kid, a young tween with reptilian scales where others might have a shaved head, skirted past me.

"Hey," I said, stopping him with a hand on his shoulder. "What is this place?"

He eyed me with distrust, glancing at my ears before deciding to answer. "Can't you read, lady? This is Wild Things." He shook off my hand and pushed through the door.

Nice kid, I thought. But then, I supposed by Mudland standards he probably was. "Nothing ventured, nothing gained," I muttered and followed him, sliding into some shadows before anyone could notice me.

What I saw, stunned.

Kids playing board games at long tables, more poring over books together. Sounding out words, slowly. Teaching each other. Helping each other. A huge court had been demarcated at one end of the wide open space where teams squared off, vying for a ball. Mirrored shards of glass had been propped against one wall where more kids practiced dance moves while a trio of boys sang in acapella and a girl kept the beat, banging on a bucket.

There wasn't an adult in sight.

A pair of boys at the long tables caught my eye, a teen quizzing an elementary schooler with flashcards. My eyes widened in recognition and I strode forward.

"Rae?" I asked, coming to stand near the boy I'd met during my first visit to the Mudlands. Bullies had corned him in the stairwell of the Gunjabmis' building – burned him, broke his bones, spat on his kem heritage. I'd saved him from anything worse, prayed he'd kept out of trouble since.

It appeared he had.

"Ms. Kozan!" He stood, dropping the flash cards in surprise.

We both knelt and started picking them up while the young pup just stared down at us openmouthed.

"What are you doing here?" we asked each other at the same time. I laughed and he blushed, his ears drooping. Not ket, I remembered. Wolven. No magic.

"I'm always here. It's kind of my thing."

"Your thing?" I asked, confused. I handed him the rest of the cards and stood, helping the awkward teen to his feet.

"Well, yeah. Here, Teddie, take these and keep practicing."

"But Rae!" he whined. "You haven't introduced us!"

"Right. Right, sorry." He laughed nervously. "Ms. Kozan, this is my little brother Teddie."

"Nice to meet you, Teddie."

"Are you really the lady who helped my brother?" he asked in a loud, awed voice.

"Yeah, I guess I am."

"Study, Teddie," Rae said tersely and started to steer me away from the tables. I noticed the other teens had started to stare at me and didn't mind leaving the area.

He took me through a kitchen area where some kids were measuring flour – baking? – and giggling. We wound up in a large office complete with standing charts and ledgers.

"Rae, what's going on?" I asked, feeling more and more confused.

"We opened two weeks ago. I couldn't stop thinking about what you'd done for me, how you'd saved me. I know you think Shari and her friends were awful, but it's what happens to kids in the Mud. We had nothing to do, nowhere to go. No one to really look after us. The schools don't care. The teachers aren't paid enough to care. I talked to my parents and some friends, and we decided to clean up this old building. The cops even helped us chase out some squatters. Now, it's a place where we can take care of our own. Whenever the schools are closed, everyone comes here to hang out. Even Shari – she's been teaching kids how to stand up to bullies, if you can believe it."

Again, he blushed.

"Are you," I paused, hardly believing it. "Dating?" I knew he'd had a crush on her, but I'd thought he was dreaming, even then.

"Sort of. Not officially, not yet. But yeah."

"Tara's toes," I exhaled, collapsing into a worn armchair. "I'm impressed, Rae. I can't believe you did all this in such a short amount of time."

"It wasn't just me," he said, scratching behind one of his tall, pointed ears.

"Still. It's pretty amazing. How do you keep the squatters and gangs from bothering you?"

"The cops come by a couple times a day. Check on the building at night, that sort of thing. We've got a couple older kids who have nowhere safe to stay, they sleep here and keep an eye on the place. It's still a work in progress, but so far, it works."

"Zee-ow, Rae! Seriously. Just. Zow. Would you mind if I told some friends? My cousins, they work with the Enso – I think they'd love to lend a hand, if you'll let them."

"Really? That would be great. A lot of the kids here are kems, but not too many kets come in. I didn't think the Circle would be interested."

"Trust me. They will be. I'll make sure of it. In the meantime, how's school going? You still thinking of joining the PGPS?"

"Maybe," he said. He shoved his hands in his pockets. "I dunno. I might want to stick around here for a while. You know, see what else we can do to help the Mudlands."

"That's cool. I'm guessing you could do a lot. I still can't believe what you've done here."

"Want a tour?" He asked, his face lighting up.

"Of course!" I exclaimed, and we spent the next hour walking the warehouse. Loft spaces on the second floor had been turned into living spaces and quiet spaces. Rae introduced me to some of the other kids, and I even shook hands with Shari, the girl who had burned Rae with a cigar the month before, just for the crime of being a kem with a crush, for daring to say hello to her in front of her friends. She had the decency to apologize and look ashamed so I decided fair was fair, apologizing for taking her and her friends out with a vicious torrent of wastewater. We all laughed, remembering the shock on their faces. I couldn't help notice the way she placed a hand on Rae's arm, the warm smile that reached her eyes.

Things really had changed here. These young kids had done what all the legislators and adults in Chalinex had failed to do: they'd come to together and started a movement. Wild Things was simple, but it was big. A school of life for the kids no one thought could be taught. Friendships forged here had the potential to shift entire timelines, change lives forever, open doors and lift hearts.

Who cared what the regs outside the Mudlands thought? Revolution was coming from the inside, grass roots growing that had the potential to fill in all the cracks in Chalinex City's pavements.

I left Wild Things on a high, soul singing and arms swinging.

I guess it was my fault.

My fault when the magic slammed into my back, knocking me to my knees. My fault when the fist rammed into my temple, rattling my teeth and almost sending me to the pavement. I should have been paying attention.

"Your bag, now!" a thin voice rasped behind me, grating every raw nerve leading into my brainstem. Hands grasped at the leather straps from behind my shoulders, invading my personal space.

It was hard to form a single thought, but I hardly needed to. My power blasted from me, unbidden but ever so needed. Wind and flame warred with each other, feeding, wanting, taking. Reclaiming my boundaries, taking back my space.

"I don't think so," I ground out, clenching my teeth as I rose painfully to my feet. The perpetrator screamed, hollered in pain, mirroring the pose I'd just climbed out of as he fell to his knees. "No one," I huffed, breathing heavily, "touches the mail." My leg shot out in an arcing roundhouse kick, my foot connecting with the mugger's chin and sending him flying back on the pavement.

I staggered over to the body, looking down.

"Shit." The thug was just a kid, looking innocent now that he was in a daze. Blood trickled from his lip where he'd bitten it.

I shook my head, grimacing against the shooting pain the movement incurred.

"Come on," I growled. I lifted him, his body thin and frail against my own. *A gods-damned kid*, I swore to myself. I poured just enough of my healing power into him to give him the strength to walk with me, but I kept his consciousness dim. I doubted it was ever any other way, anyhow. What kind of idiot attacked another ket?

The desperate kind, I imagined.

I rounded the corner, knowing Precinct 3 was nearby. The cops here had a reputation for being too lazy to do their jobs, but surely they'd be interested in a hand-delivered criminal. Besides, someone there was working with the kids from Wild Things. They couldn't all be bad.

I hauled the mugger down another block, my muscles aching in protest. Oh, to have someone of Kuma's great stature and strength with me now. But I couldn't think that way. Wouldn't think of him. Not now. I made it to the large door and pulled. Locked. Lights glimmered inside, I saw movement. How could a police station ever be locked, especially in the Mudlands? I noticed a small telephone receiver to one side, dragged the boy over, and picked up the phone.

"Hello?" I wheezed, propping the kid up against the wall and holding him there with my forearm across his clavicle.

"Nature of your business?"

"Attempted mugging. Can someone let me in? I have the perpetrator right here."

"Attempted?" The man on the other end sounded bored. "Sounds like no crime was committed."

"I'm a PGPS carrier and an agent of the CCPD. Precinct 8. You bet your sweet ass there was a crime committed."

The man chuckled and I stared at the phone, tempted to beat the receiver against the bricks. "Precinct 8, eh? Welcome to the Mudlands, honey. Look, we're understaffed today and there's no one here to process your guy. His case would probably never make it to court, anyway. We're that backed up. Violent offenders only."

"He attacked me!" I yelled.

"You bleeding?"

"No."

"Dying?"

"No, but-"

"Look, lady, you got a problem, take it up with your own damn Precinct. I got more serious shit to deal with."

And the line went dead.

"Seriously?" I hissed under my breath. The kid laughed, a soul-weary sound.

"You heard the pig. *Welcome to the Mudlands.*"

I sighed, looking the kid over. Feline eyes stared defiantly back at me.

"Look, you screwed up good, kid, but it seems this is your lucky day. I'm gonna let you go, but I'd suggest you mend your ways. Next time you attack another person, you might not be so lucky. I could have killed you, don't you get it?"

He shrugged. "I thought maybe you had some food in there. Or money. That's a nice pack you got there."

"Filled with PGPS mail, you idiot. Any other precinct would be throwing the book at you right now, you'd be going away for years. No one attacks a PGPS carrier and gets away with it."

The brat just smirked back at me.

"Right, I get it. *Welcome to the Mudlands.* Whatever." I puffed out my cheeks, thinking. "You got parents?"

"Do I look like I got parents?" he snarled.

"No, you look like a feral rat I dragged out of a trashcan," I shot back. "You need a place to stay?"

He shrugged, trying to look tough. I rolled my eyes. "Brat. Rae's not gonna thank me for this one...You heard of the Wild Things?"

"That after-school place? Bunch of goodie-two-shoe nerds."

"Not all of them," I said, thinking of Shari. "Some of those kids are just like you. And you know what? They have beds. A whole damn kitchen stocked with food. Sounds good, doesn't it?" I asked, watching his eyes dart to mine. Wary. Hungry.

"Maybe."

"Right. Maybe." I shook my head, stepping back and straightening my pack on my aching shoulders. I felt like a two-ton gorilla had pulled at the sockets there, not some half-pint hoodlum. "You should check it out. Ask for Shari, tell her Ms. Kozan sent you."

I had a feeling the girl would know just how to handle a kid like this. In fact, I bet she'd take pleasure in breaking him, the way I'd broken her. The thought of him suffering a little abuse at her hands didn't bother me one bit, not if it meant he wouldn't be mugging anyone else. Yeah, okay, and maybe my heart ached just a little bit for his situation.

Maybe.

He squinted at me like a puzzle he couldn't bring into focus, then made a face like it wasn't worth the trouble.

"You're just gonna let me go?"

I snorted. "You gonna give me another option?"

His eyebrows rose and he scooted past me, slowly, as if I might change my mind at any moment. Then, he took off, sprinting down the street.

"Wild Things!" I yelled after him. "Don't forget to ask for Shari!"

He was headed the wrong way, but I thought he just might change direction when he'd run far enough.

CHAPTER 17

games that leave bruises
words that pierce hearts – it all hurts!
let me close my eyes

I wound up at the Enso, the tiny puff of heat I pushed into the door barely qualifying as magic. The door clanked and whirred anyway, letting me in. I'd planned to stay at Jericha's, but my head was throbbing and all I wanted to do was sleep.

"Viv and Ava?" I asked the small arachnid automaton, too tired to form a full sentence as I removed my boots. I'd pulled the hood of my long sleeveless sweater over my head, hiding in my thoughts and avoiding the eyes of any passersby as I'd made my way here. Now, I yearned to wrap my mother's sweater around me like a cocoon and hibernate for several weeks. If only life could have been that simple. This was the Enso, and I had to follow protocol, even with my cousins.

The spider shuddered, crossing his arms in a gesture I took to be negative before it began backing away, beckoning me forward. I wasn't sure what it meant, but I knew I had to follow.

The fellow led me down an unfamiliar hallway, tapped on a large, ornately carved wooden door, and scurried inside.

"What is it, Spider?" a male voice asked.

I entered the room slowly, realizing it was a private study. The Arch-mage sat on a sofa, reading an ancient-looking scroll covered with strange markings. He was dressed casually in linen drawstring pants and a loose tank top.

"Arch-mage Spiren!" I exclaimed, realizing I'd barged in on the most important Arch-mage in all of Renga in his pajamas. I bowed deeply, throwing the hood over even more of my face. "My apologies, sir. I asked the robot to bring me to Viv or Ava. I never meant-"

"It's alright, youngling." I heard amusement in his voice, but I dared not look him in the eyes. Instead, I focused on the long braid he'd woven into his hair, the dark queue reaching to his waist. "Your cousins are not here, I'm afraid. I had to send them on an errand out of town and am not expecting them before evening tomorrow. Vivien mentioned you had need of her, but I reminded her that the needs of the Circle come before all else. You may, of course, use the same room as before if you would like to stay the night."

"I would, thank you, Spiren-San." My resolve to stay strong was crumbling by the minute, my limbs starting to shake from fatigue.

"Is everything all right, Kozan-kun?" he asked. The man hadn't become Arch-mage for nothing – his powers of observations were clearly still keen. I had to get out of there.

"Yes, sir. Just a long day." I ducked my head again and took a step backward.

"Alright. Spider, please escort our guest to her room. Unless you'd like something to eat first?"

"No. No, thank you." Three more steps backward.

"Sleep well, then," he said. He returned his attention to the scroll in his lap and I exhaled.

Spider led me to my room and then scuttled off to do whatever it did when no one was asking it to things. I removed my pack, placing it by the door. Then, I knelt on the tatami flooring and unrolled two plush feather beds to cover the smooth woven straw mats, one on top of the other. I stretched forward, falling into child's pose, resting my head on the floor and allowing my shoulders to slowly relax. I sighed, slowly pushing myself along the floor until my body was fully extended, prone. I turned my head to one side, breathed out slowly, and shut my eyes. Sleep came almost instantly but it didn't last.

Even before my eyes sprang open, a procession of worries marched. For everything that had gone right lately, two things had gone wrong. What would tomorrow bring?

I'd let my guard down leaving Rae's youth center and I'd paid the price, had my ass handed to me. If the kid had been bigger, if he'd landed a better shot, I could have been knocked out. Or worse. I'd been stupid, flying high and forgetting to watch my surroundings. The worse part? I knew better. I'd been taught how to stay alert in every situation, how to fight and how to track game. I'd been lectured enough times that I should never, ever have become prey myself.

But I had.

Stupid.

I punched my pillow for the fifth time, trying to get comfortable. Eventually, I gave up, bathing quietly, dressing and then slipping from the building without running into the Arch-mage or any of his steam-powered minions.

The bruise on my face had already started to fade, thanks to my ability to heal quickly, but it still looked pretty nasty. Yellow, purple and green blended together like a nebula along the right side of my temple, coloring the area around my eye and creeping up towards my hair. I could have glamoured it away or hidden it with some of Viv's makeup, but I decided not to bother. Wounds, my father had told me, should always be worn with pride, like a shield.

"Always show people you are stronger than them, that you feel no pain, and they will fear you," he'd said when I'd tried to hide my skinned knees in shame.

"But, papa, why would I want to be feared?" I'd asked, confused, climbing onto his lap. He'd smiled, taken a sip of the sake my mother had poured for him after dinner.

"You will grow into a great beauty, Nikta, I am sure, fine and fierce like your mother. Striking a little fear into the hearts of men will keep you safe, trust me. Only the bravest will dare climb your walls, only the best."

"Oh, papa, you talk funny sometimes," I'd giggled, throwing myself against him. The memory tasted of faded sunshine and sweet rice-wine. Faded, and gone too quickly, just like him.

I marched back into the Mudlands like an avenging angel, hood thrown back, coat billowing behind me in true cape fashion. I played with a ball of light as I walked, harmless but clear in its message. *This one holds power*, it said. Jonah would have killed me if he'd seen me flaunting magic this way on the streets of his city. Ava, and even Viv, too. Kets were supposed to act meek. Kets were supposed to blend in. We were most definitely not supposed to threaten the sweet, harmless regs who'd come to join us on Renga. So what if they weren't actually sweet, harmless, or even invited?

I grinned, a feral expression. Not friendly, unless you were a trout looking to sacrifice yourself to my teeth.

I walked up the stairs to the Gunjabmi's apartment, the elevator still broken, always broken. Eight wretched floors of litter and piss, but slightly cleaner than usual. I didn't want to be here, but the Gunjabmi's needed to know what was going on. If it had been Jonah, I knew I would have wanted to know, needed to hear the truth.

I knocked on the door. Waited.

The small face that answered was pale, strained. One of Henry's sisters.

"Hi. Are your grandparents home?"

She nodded, running and leaving me at the door. Not the safest or wisest of decisions in the Mudlands, but then, perhaps she'd remembered my face. I stepped inside the apartment, closing the door behind me, but went no further.

After what seemed like ages, Pablo shuffled into the room. His face looked haggard but when he saw me it lit up. "Omma," he cried, "Come quick! We have news!"

I tried to smile but found it difficult. What news did I bring? Would they find it good or bad? At least, I thought, we had an idea of where Henry might be.

Omma rushed into the room, reaching me first and grabbing my hands in her own.

"Nikta, ohalo, my dear, dear girl! You have a letter for us?"

"I don't, I'm sorry," I said, watching the smile fade from both their faces.

"Ah. Should I make some tea? How about some tea?" she said nervously, turning to fuss in the kitchenette.

"No, please. I am not hungry. I-" I paused, taking their faces in. The hope and despair, mingling together like sour plums and salt brine. "Henry never left Hokku," I blurted out.

"What?" Omma said, freezing in place. Pablo put a hand on her shoulder, though whether to steady himself or her, I could not have said.

"There is no ship. I had my police contacts check the records on Hokku – Henry never boarded any ship out of there. He arrived, but he never left."

"So, he is on the moon?" Pablo looked doubtfully at the sky outside.

"No." I bit my lip. "He is here, on Renga. Maybe even in Chalinex City."

"But, how can that be?" Omma gasped.

"He's ashamed of us? Hiding from us?" Pablo asked sadly, so quietly I thought my heart would break.

"No. He's... He was taken, we think. We're still following a couple leads."

"Taken? By who?"

"We're not sure. But there are rumors, cases Gal-Con and the police have been trying to crack for ages. They think slavers are operating out of Hokku, grabbing vulnerable kids when they pass through. Kems, mostly."

"Oh. Oh, my." Omma sank into one of the chairs around the dining table.

"He's alive though?" Pablo asked hopefully.

"We have no reason to believe he's not," I said truthfully.

Pablo nodded, looking grim, his fingers squeezing Omma's tightly.

"We'll tell Fern he's okay, that we've heard news. We'll tell her he's closer than ever before. That should make her feel better," Omma whispered, gazing up at him.

"Fern? Another of your grandchildren? I'm not sure it's wise to-"

"She's dying, wilting before our very eyes," Pablo explained. "They all are. The herbalist doesn't know what's wrong with them, but I do. Their heart is broken. They believe Henry doesn't love us anymore. Fern was closest to Henry, she became ill first. "

"Oh, no. That's terrible. Whatever you can tell her then, I guess. If it will help..." I swallowed as several tiny people crept into the room holding hands. Their eyes round and sad, their skin pale. I smiled, trying to seem kind. Trying to look reassuring.

In the low light of the apartment, they already looked like ghosts.

CHAPTER 18

push me, pull me, tell me no
where seeds lie deep, there I'll go

With Viv and Ava out of the city, I only had one option left. Bex smiled at me when I burst through the doors of Precinct 8, but my own lips tightened into a grimace.

"I need to see Pearce, now."

"Of course, right away." She looked at my face with concern. "Are you okay? That looks like it hurts."

"I'm fine. Thanks for asking."

"Right." She watched me the same way you'd look at a tiger in your living room while she spoke quietly into the phone. "Okay, you can go in, they're expecting you."

I nodded, distracted by the buzz of thoughts in my brain, and made my way through the innards of the precinct. Pearce's door was open and I spied my brother sitting inside. Two birds, one stone.

"Hi, boys," I said, breezing inside, plopping my bag on the floor and sinking into an empty chair on Jonah's left.

They gaped at me, Jonah looking shocked and worried, Lyric scowling.

"What the hell happened to you?" he growled. "I thought I warned you to keep your nose clean."

I pursed my lipped thoughtfully, rubbing my nose. "Is it dirty? Jonah, what does he mean? Do I have something on my nose?"

Jonah gaped at me like a fish.

"You know damned well what I meant, Kozan. I told you I would follow up on the leads you brought me, and I'm working on it. Your brother and I-"

"What happened to your face?" Jonah asked, seeming to come out of his stupor.

"Some idiot tried to mug me in the Mudlands. Don't worry about it, I'm fine."

"Doesn't look fine," he muttered. "Let me see."

And by let me see, he meant let me feel. He placed a hand on my bare arm and allowed our energies to mingle, to spiral around each other like twin DNA, to complete each others' twists and turns. I felt the dull ache in my head recede, but kept my eyes on Lyric's. They flickered between Jonah and I, confused, then widened as he watched the bruise on my temple begin to fade. We couldn't do much to heal everyone, not even ourselves most of the time, but Jonah and I had always been each others' salve. It was a secret we usually kept to ourselves. The bruise must have gotten worse, I must have looked really bad, or else Jonah would never have forgotten himself this way in front of his boss.

"You guys have healing abilities?" Lyric asked, sounding impressed.

"Barely," Jonah muttered. "Mostly works only on each other."

"Still pretty amazing, if you ask me."

"Yeah, well." I pushed Jonah's hand away. "That's enough. I told you, I'm fine."

"But-"

"I'm fine, Jonah," I repeated, grinding my teeth together. "I didn't come here for that."

"Fine," he said, sitting back in his seat and folding his arms over his chest. He sounded hurt. "What did you come for?"

"I came because I have a lead." I held up my hand, stopping them before they could both start yelling at me. "I know, I know, I was supposed to let it go. But I didn't, okay. I went to the Enso, and Vivien came with me to talk to Axel."

"The two of you, alone?" Lyric asked, his voice sounding strained.

Jonah snorted. "You don't know Viv. Our cousin is a force to be reckoned with, makes Nikta look like a tiger cub. Lyell – I assume he talked?"

"He did. Said he knows of only one group running slaves, and he said they're not quite slaves, either. Claimed they get 'paid', making them more like indentured servants, I guess. A fine line, to my mind, and still illegal, right?"

"Under GalCon code 387, absolutely. *No serfdoms, indenturetude or slavery shall exist. All beings shall remain free and work for fair wages*," Lyric said.

"That's what I thought," I said. "So, this group is connected with a spa down on Lilac Street, the manager, Annalee? She knows everything."

"Shit. The Blossoming?" Jonah swore, looking at his boss.

"What? What have you heard?" I asked them both.

"Too much," muttered Lyric. "It's a private spa, to all appearances completely above board. But every so often we hear things. Accusations from dissatisfied clients. Girls gone missing. Drugs. For a long time we thought they were the ones behind the feed, but when we busted Otto that theory went out the window. We've tried to set up stings, get warrants, but the judges usually turn us down."

"Yeah," agreed Jonah. "Everyone's either in the pocket of the guy who owns it, or they're scared stiff of him. No one will even say what he looks like or who he really is. Goes by a code name, Stinger. The spa itself is owned by an off-planet shell corporation, we've been trying to trace the money back to its source for over a year now, but everything's been a dead end so far."

"Okay, well now you have another lead, and an in. What's stopping you from sending in some undercover agents?"

"The Blossoming caters to regs who like kems, Nikta," Lyric said slowly. "As you've pointed out, that's something the police department is in short supply of. The few we have, well, let's just say HR wasn't too keen on us using them this way, something about discriminatory workplace practices, etcetera."

"Gee, I can't imagine. Discriminatory? The CCPD?"

"You see my point, then."

"So what? That's it? Your hands are tied? What about me? Send me in. You know I'm up for it."

"I've been considering it," Lyric admitted. This time, it was Jonah's turn to scowl.

"You wouldn't dare. You can't send her in, she's a civilian!"

"She's a CCPD agent," Lyric replied.

"And she can take care of herself," I reminded them both.

Jonah glared at my forehead pointedly. "You sure about that?"

"Yes," I huffed, crossing my legs and arms in defiance. "I am."

"Jonah, you know as well as I do that we don't know much about this guy, Stinger. But we do know he likes kems, the more exotic the better."

"She's hardly exotic," Jonah complained. "We're from settler stock, a dime a dozen."

"Maybe here. But throughout the rest of the 'verse, you're oddities. Sorry," he shrugged when I glared at his choice of words. "But it's true. Anyway, your sister is different. There's something about her…" he trailed off, looking uneasy.

"Yes?" Jonah prodded while I watched the detective with through narrowed eyes.

"She's gorgeous, okay? And that has to count for something."

Did the detective blush? He frowned at me.

"There, see, Jonah. I'm perfect."

"I didn't say that," Lyric protested, exasperated.

"Close enough. Don't worry, detective, I'm your girl. I'm all in on this."

"I still say it's a bad idea," Jonah warned.

"Look, brother. I visited the Gunjabmis before I came here. His sister is sick, maybe even dying. The grandfather's convinced it's because her heart is broken. I have to find Henry. I don't know how to explain it, but I feel like without him, they're all fading away somehow. Dying."

"It's tragic, I get it. But I don't understand how this became your problem."

"I don't know if I do, either." I reached out and took his hand in mine. "But if it was you...I'd wish for someone like us to help me."

He swallowed. "Fine. Do what you want. You will anyway. Just, promise me you'll be careful when you're in there, okay, and that you won't go off half-cocked on your own?"

I squeezed his hand, grinning. "Always."

He looked at Pearce. "You'll let me run backup on this?"

"I wouldn't expect anything less," Lyric said.

CHAPTER 19

slave body, caged heart
the truth hides behind a mask
who will let it out?

"I'll be right here the whole time," Jonah reminded me for the fifth time. He was sitting at an outdoor café across the street from The Blossoming Spa, newspaper in hand, coffee and sandwich on the table. The two bouncers across the street scanned the street constantly with their eyes, never smiling. Every so often someone would go inside. The bouncers seemed to know most of the patrons, and those they didn't were sometimes turned away. So far, only one person had come out, a portly man with a spring in his step.

"We've got backup stationed around the corner," Jonah said. "I'll give you twenty minutes. After that, we're coming in."

"That might not be enough time," I said quietly.

"It'll have to be." He'd been scowling since we'd arrived with linked arms, looking for all the world like a couple in love.

"Fine. You keep time from the minute I enter, not a moment sooner."

"Deal."

"Okay. Showtime." I slammed my own drink down, making the table shudder, and sprang to my feet. "How dare you?!"

"Nikta, I-" he protested weakly.

"Don't you 'Nikta' me! You don't think I'm attractive enough to work anywhere I want? I'll show you!" I marched across the street to the spa, where the doormen stood in front of massive flower pots. Both watched me approach from beneath hooded lids. One was smirking, so I addressed him.

"My boyfriend thinks I'm not hot enough to work in a place like The Blossoming, can you believe it? I told him, Champagne isn't good enough for me. I'm aiming big, ya know?" I placed a hand on the man's chest and gazed up into his eyes, leaning in. "What do you think? Is there room here for a gal like me?"

"For you?" The man brushed a hand down my side and I fought the urge to smack him. "I'd say so. Ditch that idiot and go on in. Ask for Annalee."

"Thanks, handsome," I purred up at him before breezing inside. I didn't spare Jonah a glance.

Inside, the spa was a maze of curtains and settees in dark corners. A bar was centrally located, where no one sat alone. I saw kems of all shapes and kinds: prowling the room in scant clothing, serving drinks at the bar, draped across patrons' laps on settees or standing between their legs at the bar, allowing themselves to be petted and pawed. Every so often I saw patrons being led upstairs by smiling kems with empty eyes. Few of the paying customers appeared to be kems themselves.

Annalee was whispering into a tall woman's ear at the bar, her fingers trailing lightly above the lady's bosom while a reptilian-skinned boy cradled her from behind. The woman blushed, throwing back her head as the young man's fingers delved into her voluminous skirts and Annalee straightened, smiling at the boy before walking away. When she caught sight of me a small pout marred the softness of her face.

"Do I know you?" she asked as she neared.

"I don't think so," I said, pretending we'd never met and giving her a wide smile. I'd temporarily darkened my hair for this mission and used makeup to re-contour my face, so I hoped she wouldn't recognize me. "I'm sure I'd remember you if we had. I was wondering if you had any job openings, maybe tending bar? I heard a friend of mine might be working here, thought I'd check it out."

"A friend, really? Who?" She looked surprised that anyone here would recommend the establishment.

"Henry. Young guy, grew up with me in the Mudlands? I used to tutor him at school."

She laughed. "I imagine Henry needed a fair amount of extra help. He's not very good at following instructions."

I chuckled, pretending I agreed. "He was terrible at math. How is he?"

Annalee examined her nails. "I couldn't say. He doesn't work here anymore. Maybe you could take his place." She looked up at me with unmasked hunger, looping an arm through mine. "Why don't you come with me to my office?"

My skin tingled. As a ket, I could tell when people were lying and this lady smelled like week-old sour milk and rotting oranges. Going somewhere private with her was the last thing I wanted to do. "Sounds great," I lied. I needed to regroup and figure out what to do. "I'd love to use the ladies room first, though. If you could steer me in the right direction?"

Annoyance washed across her face but she faked patience. "Of course, dear. The bathrooms are down that hallway. When you're finished, ask the bartender to point the way to my office." She frowned down at her blouse, tracing a finger over a minuscule stain in annoyance. "It seems I need to freshen up as well."

"Great, thank you." I tried to walk away slowly. Not run, like all my nerves were urging. Walk. When I reached the bathroom I walked straight to the counter, heart racing. Breathe, I thought. I had, what, eighteen minutes left? Seventeen? I stared into the mirror, barely recognizing myself.

Just, breathe.

The door behind me whispered open and I braced myself for an attack. A young ket walked in, glancing at me nervously. She opened a stall, peered inside. Opened another stall, checked it. Looked inside the third and final compartment.

"I heard you talking out there. You're a friend of Henry's?" she eyed me suspiciously, hugging herself around the waist. She was tiny, little more than a girl.

"Sort of. I know his family. They're worried about him."

She nodded to herself like that made sense. "They should be."

"Is he okay?" I took a step towards her and she backed away.

Again, the nod. "He's okay. But you've been lied to. He's not gone. He's upstairs, working round the clock to repay what he owes. Stinger doesn't even let him on the floor anymore, says he broke his trust," she whispered.

I swore. "Can I see him?"

"Yeah, I can take you up the back stairs. He should be alone for now. But we'll have to be quick. Come on."

I followed her out into the hallway where she looked both ways before scurrying towards a small staircase like a frightened mouse. A ket, acting like a mouse. It wasn't the strangest thing I'd ever seen, but I didn't like it.

"What's the real story with this place? How did you come to work here?" I asked.

The girl put a finger to her lips. "Quiet. We can't let anyone see you up here."

Frustrated, I complied. Again, she peered into the hall before padding lightly towards a slightly open door and pushing her way in.

"Selene, what are you doing in here? Tell Annalee I need a break, just a few more hours and then I'll-"

"Shh, keep your voice down. Someone's here to see you."

"What?" A young, thin man with a long mane of brilliant lime hair propped reclined in a rumpled bed, propping himself up on his elbows. The room smelled of sex and an alluring mixture of perfumes, overpoweringly so. "Another ket?" he groaned. "Selene, I'm not breaking in any newbies today. Tell Stinger to do it himself."

I looked at the girl, confused, and she blushed.

"Henry, you don't understand. This woman knows your family."

The young man pulled the blankets higher over his chest and scowled. "What?! Why didn't you say something? Jesus, Selene."

"It's okay," I said, stepping forward. "Selene, can you give us a minute? Maybe keep an eye out in the hall?" She nodded, looking relieved and slipped from the room. I crossed the room and drew a chair close to the bed, sitting down. The boy looked healthy enough, well fed and fit. But the smell in here... "You're turning tricks?"

His hands fisted in the sheets and he looked down, unable to meet my eyes. "My family sent you?"

"Yeah. My friends and I, we've been looking for you ever since you sent that last letter saying you were taking off. Your grandparents were worried about you. When we found out you'd never boarded a ship off Hokku, we realized slavers had probably gotten you. Henry, whatever they have you doing, it's not legal. I can get you out of here."

"And take me where?" His eyes flashed viridian in the dark room. "Home? I can't go back there, not after the things I've done. Not without enough money to take us all out of this damned place. Stinger, he knows I've got siblings. Sisters. If I even think about walking out on my contract, he said he'd take them, instead."

"Contract? You agreed to this work?"

"Not on purpose. Stinger drugged my drink, encouraged me to confide my biggest dreams, and then conned me into signing a contract promising payment in exchange for exclusive service. He makes us sign in blood and pay it back the same way, one way or another. I'm indentured until I earn my full contract price, a houseboat and stipend on Perseus – or until I die, whichever comes first." He laughed grimly.

"Look, your family is really worried about you. And Fern, she's seriously sick. All your siblings are. You need to get out of here. Forget Stinger's damned contract."

"My sister? She's really sick?"

I nodded. "Your grandfather says the herbalist doesn't know what to do. He thinks, well, he said she's heart-broken. She might die."

He chewed his lip, mulling over the information. Muttered to himself.

"Family roots run deep. If they thought I'd abandoned them... Yes, they could really get sick. Shit. I never imagined they'd be suffering. Maybe Stinger will let me see them? He's not all bad."

"If you say so," I said, shrugging, reminding him I was in the room. Henry's eyes rose to mine shyly, like a doe.

"Will you come with me to talk to him?"

"Of course. I make good backup." I spun a breeze through the room, ruffling his hair and Henry smiled, the first real one I'd seen from him.

"You have magic. Good. The other kets here, they're mostly here because they're flawed. Ket on the outside, reg on the inside. Stinger's clients like kems, but they don't want them empowered. That could be bad for business."

"Selene, too? How'd she wind up here? She's so young."

"Selene's different. She was born into the business, I guess you could say," Henry said with a grim laugh as he swung his legs over the side of the bed. The sheet started to fall away and I turned to give him some privacy. "Her mom worked here, died in childbirth. A couple of the other girls begged Stinger to let them keep her. She does the laundry, odd jobs around the spa. She's good at making herself invisible, now that some of the patrons have started to notice her."

"The mouse act? Yeah, I caught that."

"No, I mean, she can really be *invisible*. Stinger doesn't know."

"So she has powers?" I said, surprised. Looking over my shoulder. Henry had pulled on a silk kimono, loosely belter around the waist, and was brushing his hair in the mirror. "And she stays?"

"She doesn't have anywhere else to go. The orphanages here in Chalinex aren't any better. Worse, mostly. This is as good a place as any to grow up when your other choice is the Mudlands. She eats well and has dozens of people looking out for her."

"I suppose," I said, not entirely convinced, thinking of the lurid scenes she had to witness every day. And what about her schooling?

"Okay, I'm ready," he said, smoothing his long hair with one hand. "Let's go pay a visit to Stinger. He likes kets more than anything, but keep it flirty. Try to let me do most of the talking. And don't let him see your magic. It makes him tetchy."

CHAPTER 20

*clouds! green leaves shimmer silver
nature wears many faces*

"Come in," a clear alto voice called.

Henry pasted a serene look on his face and sauntered into Stinger's office. The man was good looking, pretty even. His face shone as if it had been freshly scrubbed, long hair damp and slicked back into a low ponytail at the nape of his neck. The smile on his face faded, the corners of his lips turning down into a frown.

"Henry. You're not supposed to be down on the floor."

"I know, Stinger, I'm sorry. I was hoping I could talk to you for a moment."

"Of course, dear," the man said, his eyes on me. "You know I'm always here for you."

Henry looked surprised, then noted Stinger's apparent interest in me. I had a sneaking suspicion the man was putting on a good face for me, though why I couldn't be sure.

"Right. Well, this is a friend of my family, Nikta. She's brought word that my sister was sick and I was wondering-"

"We've already met," the man said flatly, looking irritated.

"We have?" I asked, surprised. There was something familiar about him, but I couldn't imagine where I would have met a man like him.

"Yes, twice now. Though it seems you didn't want me to know that."

"I'm sorry?" I didn't understand. "I think you must be mistaken."

The man's voice went higher, the huskiness remaining. "Oh, I was wondering if you had any job openings, maybe tending bar? I heard a friend of mine might be working here."

He repeated my conversation with Annalee back to me, eyes flashing.

"But how?" And then it hit me. "You're Annalee."

The fiery hair was dulled with dampness, looking a dark brown and the face was cleaned of makeup, but that voice – I realized suddenly why the cops had been having such a hard time pinning Stinger down.

"At your service," he said with false sweetness. Then, his face turned hard. "You lied to me."

"Apologies," I said slowly. "I wasn't sure if I'd be allowed to see Henry otherwise."

"Indeed," he drawled. "You would not have been. I find familial distractions to be so, well, distracting."

"I know, sir, and I'm so sorry to even be bothering you," Henry started. "But my sister is sick. Maybe even dying. If I could just see her-"

"Out of the question," Stinger snapped. "You made a commitment."

"But his siblings – they're all sick. If they could just see him-"

"Sad, assuming you aren't both lying to me again. But I find I really don't care. Henry is one of our top earners. He can't leave."

"I don't get it," I said, genuinely perplexed. "Why are you so interested in him? Everybody else here is a kem and he's..." I trailed off, indicating how normal he seemed with a wave of my hand. Stinger laughed, a harsh, unpleasant sound, and Henry looked embarrassed.

"Why, I thought you were a friend of the family. Don't you know what he is?"

I shrugged, not sure what I was supposed to be seeing other than a good-looking guy in a kimono. Stinger snorted, reaching over and turning up the lamp on the bedside table. Illuminating the room so I could see.

Henry's skin had seemed olive-tinged in the low lighting, a factor of his heritage, I'd assumed. But it wasn't just olive -- it was olivine. In the light, I could see that his skin had a distinctly green cast.

"Your hair?"

"Natural," Henry admitted.

I hadn't noticed the tell-tale green cast to the family's dark skin before in their dimly lit apartment, had thought them simply a bit sickly, the headscarves covering their hair a nod to some religion. Now, I took in Henry's grass green eyes and hair and saw the truth staring back at me.

"You're flora?" Henry nodded, his cheeks blushing – turning greener. I'd never met a person like Henry, but I'd heard of them. Floral DNA was an old modification, one of the first chimera creations. The adaptation had allowed settlers to survive planets before the terrain could be farmed: the ability to photosynthesize meant they only needed a limited diet to provide certain nutrients. Once GalCon had gotten a handle on terraforming, the mod had fallen out of style.

"Young Henry here is a prime attraction, drawing customers like bees to honey. Did you know that the floras emit a certain, shall we say, perfume when they're aroused? It's even more intoxicating when they find pleasure. Customers can't get enough of it, and they'll do anything to keep our sweet young friend happy. Trust me, he's hardly suffering. Anyhow, Henry has broken some rules, accepting tips for customers and sending the extra money home, so now he's docked for three months and has no more communication privileges until his term is up – one more year. No pay, just play," Stinger taunted, wagging his finger at the two of us. "Now, if you want to help Henry, I can think of some ways for you to help work off his debt."

I shuddered. "Thanks, but no." I turned to Henry. "Is this true? Did you take money you shouldn't have?"

"Well, yes, but, it was my sister's birthday and I didn't think it would hurt anyone. It wasn't like I stole the money, they were my tips," he said.

"Tips you aren't allowed to encourage or keep. You were given ample time to read and understand your contract before you signed on here. No one forced you-"

"I was drunk. I didn't understand anything!" Henry ground out, turning on Stinger.

"Not my fault you can't handle your wine," the boss laughed, clearly not feeling bad for Henry at all. He let down his hair, ruffling the damp strands with his fingers, taking on a more feminine air. "He's no innocent. We have an ironclad agreement. If he leaves here with you, he'll never get a penny of the money he's earned. I will punish his entire family."

"Is that a threat?" I hissed. I knew I had only a few minutes left before Jonah came to storm the castle.

"Just a fact," he said, preening. "I'm the queen bee here, and no one leaves this hive without permission. Not unless they want to feel my sting."

"You would harm children? Old people? What kind of monster are you?"

Stinger lifted one shoulder delicately. "I know where the Gunjabmi's live. Know everything about them. Where do you think they will go, how do you think they will improve their circumstances, without the money Henry has saved?"

I shook my head. "Anywhere would be better than here."

"Don't bet on it," he snarled.

Angry, I raised my hands, allowing them to fill with fire. Wind rose, sending all our hair billowing. "You can't own people," I growled.

"My, my, the cat has claws." Stinger clapped his hands, delighted. Not scared. "Henry, put a leash on your friend."

I felt a hand on my shoulder. "You don't have to stay here," I said, not looking at him.

"I do," he said sadly. "Please, don't cause more trouble."

"Henry, you can't-"

"I have to. Please. Just go. Tell my family I'm okay. Tell them anything. Just don't," his voice caught. "Don't tell them where I am. What I'm doing. They can't know."

The quiet sadness in his voice got to me. I clenched my fists, letting the fire die, extinguishing hope.

CHAPTER 21

opportunities
slip through open fingertips
clutch tight, lose it all

Jonah was just getting up from the table across the street when I exited the spa.

"Talk about cutting it close. I was about to signal the other team and come get you," Jonah said, looking me over carefully. "How did it go?"

"Not good," I sighed. "Can we walk and talk?"

"Sure, let's tell the backup team we're wrapping up. I've gotta get back to the precinct, anyhow. Tell me everything."

I vented as I walked, looking over my shoulder occasionally to make sure we weren't being followed. "So, they won't let him out at all, not even to see his sister for a couple of hours," I concluded.

"Shit," Jonah said, stopping next to an unmarked delivery truck. He motioned to the driver, signaling them with a hand across his neck that the operation had been called off. "That's heavy. I'm not sure what we can do, considering there's a legal contract. It's not slavery."

"Not even if he was drugged or coerced into signing the documents?"

"We'd have to prove it, and it's Stinger's word against Henry's. I still can't believe no one realized Stinger and Annalee were the same person. Gender-fluid. How could I have missed it? I feel like an idiot."

"Not an idiot. Maybe a bit blind. We see what we want to. Besides, it's an amazing changeover, I'm not sure I would have caught on if they hadn't revealed the truth to me themselves. Either way, they're gorgeous."

"A gorgeous criminal," Jonah retorted. "Maybe there's something in their past we can get them for, something else they've managed to keep hidden. But how do I even do a background check? Was Stinger born a woman? A man?"

"No idea. That's your wheelhouse. I guess look for both – maybe research twins links to crimes? They could have passed themselves off as two siblings, a couple, who knows? Keep in mind, too, that Stinger is a nickname. Queen bee, they called themselves, ruler of the hive. Their employees know the truth. Maybe someone knows more."

"Maybe. We could try sending someone in undercover."

"That might work," I agreed. "Or maybe you can get them on child endangerment or labor laws? Selene's too young to be working, I'm sure of it. And a brothel isn't a place anyone should have to grow up in."

"I don't know. Knowing Stinger, they probably have guardianship papers for the girl. But you're right – child services might be interested. I'll check into it. You want a ride anywhere, back to the precinct or something?"

"No. I should head back to Prime. Letters to deliver and all that. You'll call if anything comes up?"

"Count on it." He wrapped his arms around me, taking me off guard. After a moment, I hugged him back, hard. "You take care out there, eh Nikta?"

"You, too, brother. Ohalo." I squeezed him one last time.

"Ohalo, big sister," he grinned, ruffling my hair before turning away and climbing into the truck.

I headed straight to the mountains, seeking the clarity of a higher viewpoint. The stars usually made me feel expansive but tonight they made me feel small. Powerless. I'd wanted to help the Gunjabmis so badly, and now I didn't know what to do. Worse, I couldn't get Selene off my mind.

I made camp on a rocky outcrop; tried to meditate, to clear my brain of thoughts.

It didn't work. I pulled a piece of scrap paper from my pack and started on a flow of consciousness, trying to exorcise the demons from my head by naming them.

When I had finished, I realized what I'd written was a poem to Kuma. I hadn't even realized he was on my mind. In my heart. I re-read the words, each one lifting the barest weight from my chest.

family tugs my heart, tabletop games
sisters, brothers, grandparents kept apart
connections broken, wounds and scars that maim

everyone wants to be loved, everyone
everyone wants to be free, everyone

i don't have the right words to make you mine
yours, his, theirs, ours, all hearts converge as one
how can i choose just one beat, tick-tock, chime?

everyone wants to be found, everyone
everyone wants to be saved, everyone

hello, goodbye, ohalo, aho-em
blessings to you, blessings to them

my heart beats for wilds no lyrics can tame

So much truth, a modicum of clarity. Part of me yearned for Kuma, but nothing had changed. I had no space, no tick-tock time in my heart for a significant relationship right now. Things with Jonah were improving and my work with the CCPD had taken me down a new road. All consuming, scary at times, and immeasurably rewarding. So many beating hearts needing my help, how could I answer only his call? When he finished his walkabout, I knew he would want to return to his home, with or without me. I'd told him I would never leave Renga, leave what little was left of my family. But that wasn't all. The truth was, I was scared of being tamed, scared of being tied down. Kuma had hinted he would wait, but his letter to me had been filled with double meanings, hard to read and shooting daggers into my heart. He said he was mine, but he was clearly mad he'd been sent away. A true bear, Kuma needed commitment, a mate. And I wasn't there yet. I wasn't sure I ever would be.

I stared at the sonnet, a form I rarely used. I'd missed a line, but I liked the flow of the poem, didn't care to fix it. The flaw would drive the professor in Kuma crazy.

If I sent it, I might never see him again.

If I didn't, what else would I write? I could detail the case I was working, talk about the beauty of the wilds. Avoid a serious heart-to-heart. I pulled his own letter from my pack, smoothed out the crumpled paper and compared the two letters side by side.

He hadn't provided a return address, but he'd listed a city, Kyogamura. I could send the poem general delivery. If he received it, whatever happened was fate. Amarasu would see to that, wouldn't she? I had to trust the patron of lovers, homes and hearts to know what was best.

Quickly, I scrawled only my name below the poem. Once rolled, the letter fit neatly into one of the small, spare mail tubes I usually carried. I said a quick prayer to Amarasu, lifting the tube into the air in a display of wind and light. When I was thru, I caught the tube in my hands and addressed it in careful, clear lettering before putting it back into my pack with other letters destined for the Prime sorting facility.

Kokuma Matsui, General Delivery, Kyogamura, Corun Province, Renga.

Connection made, connection severed. It was in the gods' hands now.

CHAPTER 22

cat pounces and leaps – daring!
friends join, chasing hares, claws sheathed

"Pickled kumquats?"

Francine Sumisu placed a small bowl in front of me on the kitchen table, already knowing the answer. Jericha's mother had been like my own growing up and she knew I couldn't resist the combination of sweetness and tart citrus. She poured me a glass of cool water and sat down, plucking one of the orange treasures and placing it on her own tongue, clucking delightedly.

"I never tire of these," she said.

"Nor I," I agreed. I'd stopped at Francine's first thing upon my arrival in Prime. Jericha had asked me to carry some yendar home to her mother, the extra currency always welcome now that Francine had retired from teaching. She had a pension, but it barely covered her monthly bills. She supplemented her income now with piecework, sewing by lamplight, and Jericha's thoughtfulness was always appreciated. I also dropped things off from time to time – not money, she never would have accepted that from me, but sweet cakes, finely smoked fish, perfumed soaps. Today, however, I brought only Jericha's boon.

"Something's troubling you dear, what is it?" she asked, eying me thoughtfully.

"I was just thinking I didn't bring you anything," I admitted.

"Not that," she disagreed. "Something else. Besides, you know you don't ever have to bring me anything. Just yourself."

She patted my hand, eyes sparkling. She'd always been so kind.

And, she always knew when I was hiding something. An empath, she could feel the emotions of other people – when they were lying, scared, worried, happy. The ability had served her well as a school teacher and kept Jericha and me out of trouble more than once.

"I wasn't even thinking about my woes," I lamented. "How do you do that?"

"How does Hokku rise each morning?" She shrugged. "Only Buddha knows why we have each been granted the powers we have. Sometimes, it's been as much a curse as it has been a blessing."

My mouth must have dropped open because she laughed and gently closed it with one finger. "But I thought being an empath made you so, so wise!"

"Maybe. But it also scared away more than one suitor in my youth. And some I thought were friends, too. It hasn't always been easy."

"At least you never have to waste time figuring out what people feel," I muttered.

"Ah!" she laughed. "So it's man troubles, is it? The wild Nikta has finally found a tom she admires?"

"No," I grumbled. "Quite the opposite, it appears. Anyway, that's not what's worrying me, not really."

She looked skeptical, so I launched into a lengthy explanation of what was going on with the Gunjabmi family, how I'd gotten involved, and the dilemma I faced on getting Henry out. Francie, having been the mother of a young girl herself, seemed most worried about Fern and Selene.

"Henry has gotten himself into a real pickle, made some bad decisions. No parent would ever want their child to be in his situation, but he *is* an adult. Those poor girls, though. They did nothing to deserve what they're going through."

"I know. Everyone wants to help, but it's all going too slowly for me. I hated leaving the city knowing anything could happen while I am gone. Things could go from bad to worse so easily."

"Indeed. So what will you do?"

"I have no idea."

"You'll figure it out. You always do. Pray to Tara, she will help you."

"I feel like prayers are all I do anymore." I stared down into my glass, Yuki's white orb dancing across its surface. It was the twenty-fourth day of Cat. In three days, a new month would dawn. Sakura would rise, bringing Rabbit's caution into play. It had been sixteen days, hardly more than a week since I'd first promised the Gunjabmi's I would look into Henry's disappearance, yet I was no closer to bringing him home. I frowned and finished my water.

"I should go. I have some things I need to get to Florence."

Francine walked me to the door, wrapped me in a soft hug. "Things will work out. You'll see. You take too much responsibility for everyone in your life. Play a little, stay in touch with your wild side."

"Believe me, I'm trying. Ohalo, Francie."

"Ohalo, sweet girl. Give my daughter a kiss next time you see her!" she called after me.

"Two kisses, I promise!" I turned and jogged off, heading towards the PGPS.

At the back gates of the mail headquarters, a familiar face broke into a smile.

"Why Nikta, you dog! Where have you been? I can't believe you snuck out on us like that." She swatted at me playfully, then took my pack and handed it to the new sniffer behind her.

"Sneak? I told Sheila I was going."

Paisley pouted. "That is so not the point."

"I'll make it up to you guys. Dinner at my place next week?"

The man finished his examination of every pocket and piece of mail before handing my pack back to Paisley, who in turn gave it back to me.

"You can count on it. You'll cook salmon?"

"Sure."

"With your homegrown Meyer lemon sauce?"

"Absolutely. Sticky rice and a raspberry tart?" I knew what Paisley liked.

She moaned. "You're killing me. Yes! Yes to all of it."

"Great. Eighth Rabbit? I should be around then."

"It's a date. Let me know if something comes up."

"Deal. Give Sheila my love." I pecked her on the cheek and strode past the second set of gates into the sorting area.

I snuck up behind Florence and placed my hands over her eyes.

"Nikta Kozan, I'd know you anywhere," she grinned.

We hugged and I dumped out my deliveries on her table.

"Zee-ow, that's a lot you were carrying," she exclaimed.

"Tell me about it. I took a few more breaks than usual, basically every time my shoulder started to go numb."

"What's this?" She had picked up one of the returned packages from the Seekers, puzzling over the address. "Didn't I send these out with you for delivery?"

"You did. The compound is walled off now, complete with armed sentries. They wouldn't let me in to see the recipients and they wouldn't send them out to receive their packages personally."

"But that's crazy. Everyone knows the carry-with-cares have to be signed for in person. It's been standard procedure for oh, four hundred years now everywhere in the galaxy."

"I know. I tried to reason with them but they have a strict 'no kem' policy, even for the PGPS."

Flo swore. "Those racist bastards. Well, they're gonna find it real difficult to do otherwise. I don't think I have a single reg who's gonna be able to do that route in, oh, shall we say ever?"

I chuckled, knowing she meant it. The only thing Florence hated worse than mail bandits was a reg bigot.

"Why, I think even the class B mail truck out that way is being manned by several kets. Real big ears, those fellows have. The biggest. Trucks been having some mechanical issues, too. I sure do hope nothing happens to delay their scheduled deliveries. That would be a real shame," she tutted.

"It surely would," I agreed. "Almost as much of a shame as them laying claim to Aligna's Well."

Florence gasped. "They wouldn't."

"They did. Put their wall right around the entire compound, well and all. And get this – they're charging thirty yendar a visit. To non-kets, of course. People like you and me, we can't even look at it."

Florence sputtered. "Why, I never! People are gonna hear about this. Claiming Aligna's Well, the nerve."

"Yeah, I reported it to the Enso in Chalinex, but they said there wasn't much they could do."

"No, of course not. This is an issue for the Puraimura authorities." She patted my arm. "Don't you worry. We'll get this sorted. That, or they can kiss their rights to mail goodbye."

"Can you do that?" The right to mail was considered an inalienable right, protected under GalCon law.

"I have ways." She winked at me and returned her attention to the pile in front of her. "Anything else here I need to know about?"

"Just one." I handed her my letter to Kokuma.

"Kokuma Matsui." She raised her eyes to mine. "Little Bear? Interesting name. Don't see much general delivery anymore."

"He's here on walkabout, I'm not sure he'll even be there, but-"

Understanding dawned across her face. "Is this for that professor fellow? He was a bear, wasn't he?"

I nodded, blushing.

"Say no more. I know the head of the office there, I'll attach a note, make sure she finds out if he's been through already. If he has, Meskin will find out where he's headed. She gets the goods on everybody who passes through Kyoga – she'll get it to him, wherever he is."

"Amarasu willing. I'm not sure I even want to hear back from him," I said, my cheeks still burning.

"Speaking of strapping men," Florence started. "I heard you put on a real show with Cadence McRory's son a few nights back."

"You heard about that?" I cringed.

"Honey, the whole town heard about it."

"Right. Well. It was nothing. Just something we put together for the show."

"That's not what I heard," she teased.

"Nothing happened." *This time*, I thought. I really needed to change the subject. "You have my route ready?"

"Of course, hold on." She walked over to another part of her vast table, picked up a basket of letters and handed it to me. "Just a few things this time."

"Okay, great. My shoulders thank you," I said, meaning it. "Oh, Mrs. Herold, good. I haven't seen her in a while."

"Tell the old bird I say hello," Florence grinned. "And that I miss our long talks."

"She does know how to talk. Alright, I guess that's it then. I've got some things going on in Chalinex, I'll probably be heading back out again at first light."

"Things? A case?" Florence wrinkled her nose. I knew she didn't like me working with the police department, that she worried for my safety.

"Sort of. More of a personal favor I'm doing for a friend. I can't really get into it." I didn't want to upset Florence, and I knew how she'd feel about me visiting a brothel. If she knew the establishment also ran on indenturement? I never would have heard the end of it, how she'd promised my family she'd look after me, how I'd added another furrow to her brow. No, it was better not to drag her into my troubles.

She was, of course, to keen to evade. "You can't fool me. You're in some kind of trouble, or someone else is. Never mind, you'll tell me when you're ready. Just try not to get yourself blown up again, okay? Your grandfather-"

"I know, I know."

"Do you? Onkoro Wakanazu was my mentor, one of the finest men to ever grace this branch. When I go to the temples at Matsuri, I light joss for him, too, and your mother and father."

"Oh, Florence, I had no idea." Moved, I bowed my head in respect. "You do my family a great honor. I will not disappoint you. Any of you."

She sighed. "You couldn't even if you tried."

Knowing the storm had passed, I grinned and scooped the mail into my bag along with my route map, taking advantage of the moment to leave before she could change her mind and berate me some more.

"I promise, I'm not trying. You're the best, Flo, really. See you in Rabbit!"

She rolled her eyes, teasing. "Not if I see you first!"

CHAPTER 23

empty eggless nests
ewes bleat in fallow meadows
surprise! harvest waits

After a solid night of sleep and more than a day's travel through the wilds, I emerged from the forest onto the small lane that led to Herold Homestead. I could have taken Route 8 almost the entire way from Prime, a much more direct route, but I always preferred to stick to the wilds, avoiding traffic and bandits. Besides, I'd heard the road had been partially washed out weeks ago and doubted it had been repaired yet.

The woods along the dirt road to Mrs. Herold's quickly gave way to pastoral scenes. Wide, rolling meadows bordered by thorny hedgerows even the most ornery goat wouldn't touch. Fields of grain. Three barns, two silos, a lackadaisical windmill and a large array for collecting galactic radiation to heat water for the house. The home itself was a sprawling thing that had grown almost of its own will over the years; an amalgamation of quick-crete domes, mud-brick extensions and gold-mirrored glass.

Mrs. Herold was a widowed homesteader whose son had run off for the bright lights of Hokku over a year ago, leaving her to take care of the farm on her own. She hired seasonal help whenever she could, but I knew she was lonely for company. Even when her husband and son had been around, she'd been notorious among runners for talking your ears off. Now, she'd start preparing tea and fresh rice cakes the moment she heard you coming down her lane. A large mixed-herd of goats and sheep had already been bleating at me for three minutes, so I figured she'd had fair warning by the time I mounted the steps to her front porch.

I raised my hand to knock on the door but touched only air as the wooden panel swung open. Mrs. Herold stood in the opening holding a tray of iced green tea, two glasses and an assortment of sweet and savory rice balls. She greeted me on sight.

"Miss Kozan, dear, how nice to see you. I suppose you've come with a letter from Ned?" she said, bustling past me.

Her son, not being all bad, sent her home money every couple months to help support the farm. I considered it a fair trade, since she always had to hire help to do the work she couldn't keep up with without him. No one was supposed to know what came in his letters, but Mrs. Herold wasn't very good at keeping secrets.

"Yes, I have it right here." I followed her to a small table on the covered porch and set the padded envelope down next to the tray, along with my signature pad. Familiar with the carry-with-care routine, she signed for the delivery and then motioned for me to sit down, settling into a wicker chair across the table from me.

"So, tell me, young lady, how is life treating you? Found any beaus you want to tie yet?" She cackled, delighted at her own joke, and poured us each a glass of tea.

I chuckled and shook my head. "No, can't say I have." Kuma and Innis barely even registered in my thoughts, a welcome reprieve.

"Ah, to be young again, the world at my fingertips. I tell you what, these old bones just aren't getting around like they used to. Thank goodness the wood is all cut and the tractor is ready to go for harvest next week, 'cause that amaranth won't cut itself."

"Where's the new farmhand? Steve? Sean?" I couldn't remember the man's name from the month before when she'd pointed him out to me where he'd been brushing the cashmere goats to collect the valuable fibers. The sheep were used for milking, a short-haired variety that produced no wool, while the goats were kept for meat and textile production, the yarns and loomed fabrics gaining a pretty penny at market.

"Scott. The bastard ran off last week with two of my prize does and a buck. If he'd just asked, I would have given him the goats in exchange for working the harvest, but no. He just up and left."

"That's terrible, I'm so sorry."

"Just disappointing, is all. Things will work out, they always do."

"Are you going to report him to the police?"

"What's the point? Ain't nobody got time for that. Naw. I'll just pray Tara sends some itinerants my way, and if she doesn't I'll do the work myself."

I looked at her, taking in the knotted knuckles and weathered skin. "That's a lot of work for one person. Do you ever think about giving up the farm. Retiring?"

"Me? Never! Pop left me plenty of money to keep things going, even without my Ned. Naw. I love the work. Keeps me young, gives me something to live for. Most of my friends have passed on and you know what I think?"

I shook my head.

"They was just plum bored. Saw their families grown, retired, and then they had nothing to do. The spirit withers away when a body has nothing to do, my daddy always said so and I believe him. Now me, you take me, I might wish for some conversating now and again to pass the hours, but I keep busy. After the planting is done, I walk the fields each day to check on my babies, the plants, you see? I count the herds each morning and night, work on my loom when my hands fall idle, pray to Tara and Amarasu while I work. I haven't had a prayer fall on deaf ears yet, neither. All my prayers are answered, always. Sometimes it just takes a while for the blessings to find their way here, is all, but I don't fret. I know I live a ways out, that my lane is long and winding. Some blessings come slower than others, but they all walk the same trail, and they always find me."

"Why, Mrs. Herold, I do think you have a bit of the poet's spirit in you. What a beautiful way to put things. I'm glad you're happy, I worry about you sometimes, you know. Out here all by yourself."

"Not entirely alone," she half-whispered, half-sang. "I've got Betsy."

"Betsy?"

She grinned and rose from the table, going inside for a moment and returning with a heavy shotgun. My eyes widened and I leaned back instinctively.

"Miss Kozan, meet Betsy." She pumped the gun and aimed down the lane. "We girls got to stick together." Again, she cackled, pulling the trigger. A puff of dirt exploded in the distance. "Take that, you no-good mangy thief!"

"Huh. Guess I don't have to worry about you after all." I'd never been a fan of guns, but I was glad Mrs. Herold had herself some backup on the farm.

"I should say not," she agreed, returning the shotgun to its resting place inside the door. Once more, she sat at the table, taking a prim sip of tea. No one would have ever guessed she'd just been pretending to shoot

Scott's balls off down the lane. "I just wish I had some good company sometimes, is all. Betsy always helps entertain me when I'm feeling ornery, and my ewes are sweet as pie, but they don't add nothing the conversation during milking. Onigiri?"

Used to the way Mrs. Herold often switched topics mid-stream, I had no trouble accepting her offer.

"Thank you, yes." I grabbed one of the seaweed wrapped rice balls and took a careful bite, savoring the sweet miso and red bean filling. "Delicious, as always."

We chatted for a couple more hours. I managed to excuse myself gracefully in under three, which had to be a new record: most runners found themselves staying the night at the Herold Homestead, but I'd mastered the art of the polite exit. The trick, I'd found, was to plead deadlines just after we cleared the table, when her hands were deep in suds, washing up.

As always, she insisted on giving me something for the road, pressing the small, waxed-fabric wrapped package into my hands. "It's a new recipe I've been working on, aged brie laced with veins of crystallized honey. You let me know how it is."

"I will, thank you so much. I'm so sorry to run like this, but-"

"Duty calls, I know. Letters to deliver, young bucks to bump."

I blushed. "Mrs. Herold!"

She laughed heartily and pushed me out the door. "Go on with you now, git. And if you see any strapping men looking for work, you send them my way, hear?"

"I will, thank you."

Well-fed and feeling happier than I had in days, I took off in an easy jog through one of the fields, back into the wilds. Sakura's rosy round face had risen, marking the start of Rabbit, casting a warm glow over the fields. I had one more delivery to make before reaching Chalinex City, one more day of hard travel before I reached city limits, and an idea had begun to form in my mind.

CHAPTER 24

hare stomps its foot, ready
time to play! call the warren

I took more care journeying through the woods after I left Mrs. Herold's, knowing my powers were at a low point with Sakura's rising. That night, I wrote poems to each of my ancestors, welcoming them back in my own small, private kami-mukae ceremony to welcome the return of the gods and spirits. Then, I danced, whispering my prayers for the living: safety for Henry, happiness for the Gunjabmi's, abundance for the Sumisu's, support for Mrs. Herold. Continued rehabilitation for the Mudlands, a strengthening of the bond between me and Jonah.

Rabbit had risen, the totem of community. It was said Rabbit heard all, knew all, and used that knowledge for the betterment of the warren. For the tribe. Of course, rabbit could also jump into action before thinking things through and it had a nervous disposition, ready to run and hide at any loud noise. I would have to proceed more carefully this month and stay centered. Overall, though, I considered the new month to be a good omen. An auspicious month for families to come together, surely.

With rabbit in mind, I went straight to the Enso after dropping off my last delivery. The halls of the magical headquarters were eerily quiet, spider weaving its way through them like a maze, taking me to a section I'd never visited before. The mech scuttled up the wall beside a door, something I hadn't realized it could do, creeping me out more than usual. When it reached the lintel at the top, the automaton went through a series of movements, almost as if it was doing martial arts. As it performed one last flying kick, the gears within the door spun, folding the barrier into itself, and I was blasted with a wall of heat that almost knocked me off my feet.

"Shit, sorry!" Viv exclaimed, rushing towards me. "I wasn't expecting you to be there. No one except Spiren and Spider can get in when I'm training."

I looked around, dazed, as she took hold of my elbow and led me into the middle of the large, empty room.

"Spiren spelled this place just for me last week, after I set the mats in the main training room on fire again. Cool, right?"

I didn't miss the sarcasm in her voice. Now that she wasn't actively training, the temperature in the room was dropping fast. The entire room was made of metal

– metal that was now building layers of ice upon every surface.

"Zow. I've never seen anything like this."

"Yeah. Spiren's got talent, I'll give him that. Even if he is one hell of a frosty beast sometimes." She laughed when I shivered involuntarily. "See what I mean? If he can make it this cold on the outside, what must he be like on the inside? Come on, let's get you warmed up."

Teeth chattering now, I was happy to let her take my hand and lead me from the room. Sitting in the kitchen, a cup of hot tea in my hands, I started to warm up again.

"Well, that's one way to keep you motivated," I said with a grin.

"Tell me about it. I have to practice having enough control not to immolate myself while targeting my enemies and not freezing, all at the same time. It's even harder this time of month, with Sakura messing with my energy flow. Spiren's calculated the rate of cooling just perfectly so that if I don't produce flames at just the right level, I'll go into hypothermia."

"He doesn't go easy on you guys. I thought working at the Enso was a cushy gig, but now I'm thinking not so much."

Viv giggled. "It's not that bad. I'm just feeling prickly after the scolding he gave me last week. Anyhow. You didn't come here to hear me complain. How are you, cousin?"

"Well enough, but I'm done playing games," I said. I launched into an explanation of everything I'd found out about Annalee – Stinger – and Henry's situation since I'd seen her. "Fern is dying. Henry is miserable. I don't care if his contract is legally binding. It's time to get him out."

"But you said Stinger will go after his family?"

"That's what he said. But I have an idea about that, too." I laid out my plan. "Will you help me?"

"Are you kidding? You want me to choose between freezing my assets off and leaping head first into danger? Hmm, let me think about it..." She tapped her chin, quirking her lips. "Family first, rabbit tells us. I'm in, of course."

"Should we get Ava, too?"

Viv shook her head, putting her dishes in the sink. "No, she and the Arch-mage went out to some meeting with the mayor. I wasn't invited," she said, sticking out her tongue and making a face.

"Probably wise," I said, laughing as I rose to my feet.

"Probably," she agreed. "Besides, this is going to be way more fun. You ready to do this?"

"Past ready. Let's go."

When we got near the spa, Viv glamoured me to look like Ava, just in case the bouncer had been given orders not to let me in again. She needn't have bothered. The guards at the door were different, men I'd never seen before, and they practically drooled on Viv as she flirted with them to gain entrance. I stood back, arms folded and looking bored, cool as ice, just like Ava would have been had she really been here.

Inside, she dropped the glamour and I shifted the air around us to bend the light. This time of the month, it was about all I could manage, a glamour well beyond my reserves. We weren't invisible, exactly, but we'd be harder to see among the dim, curtained room. We climbed the stairs, heading straight for Henry. When I pushed the door to his room open, I found a man and woman fawning over him, the woman cradling his head between her breasts, trailing her tongue over his ear; the man caressing his legs, nuzzling one thigh.

"Mmm, Henry, you smell sooo good," the man whispered and the woman moaned in agreement. Henry's eyes were closed, head thrown back. He didn't seem to be hating this. The floral scent in the room was heady. Not a perfume, as I'd assumed before, but Henry himself. "See what you're doing to my wife? Your pleasure is our pleasure," the man said, his breath coming in gasps now.

"Hate to interrupt the party, folks, but..." Viv trailed off, muttering something under her breath and screwing up her eyes. I felt a slight pressure behind my eyes and staggered back, while the three people on the bed collapsed into unconsciousness.

"What the hell did you do?" I hissed, rushing forward.

"Just a little something Ava and I have been working on. Ava's way better at it than I am, obviously. But it worked, didn't it?"

"How are we going to get Henry out of here if he can't walk?"

"Stop fussing. I just made a little suggestion to them, that's all, a sort of telepathic push. I should be able to wake him up."

"Should?" I ground my teeth together. This was just the sort of impetuous behavior rabbit warned against. Still, I tried to be patient while Viv worked, pushing the man off of Henry and then placing her hands over his cheeks, whispering once more.

Nothing happened.

I swore, stepping forward, trying to channel some of my healing energy into the soles of his feet while she worked. Finally, after minutes that felt like hours, his eyes fluttered open.

Widened, seeing us. His cheeks flared the color of moss and he sprang from the bed, wrapping a kimono around him.

"A little late for that, don't you think?" Viv drawled.

Henry ignored her. "Nikta, you shouldn't be here. Stinger was really pissed last time. He threatened to extend my punishment."

"Your punishment is over, Henry. We're getting you out of here. You, and Selene," I added.

"Selene?" Viv said, surprised. "Who's that? You never mentioned anyone else."

"You'll see. Henry? Where is she? Think, we've got to move quickly."

"I can't leave, you know that," he protested sullenly.

"You damned well can," Viv said hotly. "I'm here as a representative of the Arch-mage and I say your contract is up. Now listen to my cousin and get moving."

I watched the hope dawn on his face. "You're serious?"

"Tara's toes!" Viv exclaimed, then dropped her voice to a whisper as the man murmured in his sleep behind us. "Yes, we're serious. Grab your things and let's go."

Henry scanned the room, grabbed a small wooden box, and turned. "My family's letters and this week's tips. There's nothing else here for me."

"Wise boy," Viv said, and peeked into the hallway. "Coast is clear. Come on." She draped herself over Henry like a besotted client. "Wrap your arm around my waist, just in case we run into anyone," she instructed him. "Lead the way."

"She's probably prepping tonight's aids," he said, thinking. "Stinger doesn't trust the rest of us to handle it."

He led us further down the hall to a small room filled with stacks of white envelopes. "A mail room? I don't understand."

Selene sat at a small desk, wrapping each envelope with a pretty golden bow. The beautified envelopes were then placed in small baskets, each one a gift begging to be opened. I picked up one of the baskets from its shelf on the wall and examined it, eyes widening in surprise when I recognized what it held.

"The feed? Stinger still has a supplier?"

Selene shook her head. "Cops busted our production team last month. This is the last of our inventory."

Another surprise. "You're saying Stinger was the mastermind behind the feed? He was Otto's boss?"

"Yeah. Annalee's been on the warpath ever since Otto ran off with her kitchen witch," Henry said.

I gazed around the room. I was glad to hear she had no idea we'd placed Bartholomew into witness protection, but there were still hundreds, no thousands, of letters here. Each one represented a dose of the feed. Thousands of doses, each one a step down the road to addiction, apathy, and death. "Plan's changed, folks. We can't just leave this stuff lying around."

"We can't take it with us, either. Want me to burn it?" Viv asked, rubbing her hands together in anticipation.

Selene blanched and scrambled to my side. "No," I said. "Too dangerous. We'll let the cops handle it, give our friends in blue something to do. Selene, do you have a phone around here?"

"Yes, at the end of the hall."

"Show me."

We followed the young ket to a tiny, curtained alcove and crowded inside. "Stinger lets some of us call home, you know, when we do good. I don't have any family, but I have the code, just in case one of the customers gets rough or there's an emergency," she explained, chattering as she picked up the phone and dialed a few digits. Viv met my eyes over the girl's head. I wasn't a telepath, but I knew what she was thinking. Selene was only a child. She didn't belong here, surrounded by drugs and sex. "Here, you can dial out now."

"I didn't know you had the code," Henry whispered, sounding hurt as I dialed Lyric's direct line. Selene shrugged and looked at the ground. What could she say? She'd been just as much a prisoner of Stinger's whims as anyone else. Perhaps more so, with no contract, no family, no way out.

"Pearce," Lyric answered curtly.

"Lyric," I breathed in relief. "Nikta Kozan. Listen, I only have a minute. You need to get a squad to the Blossoming Spa right away. They have an entire storeroom of the feed on the second floor, sixth room on the right."

"And you know this how?"

"I was just standing in it."

The detective swore.

"Get out of there, now."

"We're leaving. Just, this isn't only a stockpile – it's *the* stockpile. Stinger, Annalee, whatever – they were the mastermind behind the whole thing. Stinger's the boss you've been looking for."

"Fuck. Noted," he said tersely and hung up.

"They're on their way. Come on."

I started for the hall, stopped when I heard giggles and the sound of a hand smacking skin.

"We've got company. Viv, can you wrangle up another glamour for all of us?"

"Sure, what are you thinking?"

"Make Henry and Selene look like that couple from the room. I'll play Ava again, might as well stick with what works."

"Okay, let's go."

My skin tingled as Vivien's glamour settled over us. Henry looked down at his now distended belly in distaste, while Selene played with the gold band that had appeared on her finger, looking pleased.

"Perfect. This is it. Selene, you're with me."

"Claraline," Henry corrected. "She's Claraline, and I'm Andre."

"Right," I nodded and threaded Selene's arm through mine. We threw the door open, acting drunk. "That's not the bathroom!" I exclaimed and pretended to stumble into the hall. The pair several doors down didn't bother looking up, too busy locking lips.

I ignored the urge to cover Selene's eyes with my hand, guessing she'd seen worse and that Claraline wouldn't need to be shielded from anything. No. The woman had come here with her husband to see everything. Feel everything. I tried to keep the disgust I felt off my face as we traipsed towards the stairs.

We were crossing the main floor of the spa when Annalee spotted us, bestowing a wide smile on the husband and wife. When her eyes roamed over my face, however, the smile faded. She'd met Viv and Ava at the gala, knew they were Enso.

She excused herself from her guests and walked towards us purposefully, pasting a welcoming expression on her face to try and hide cold eyes.

"Andre, Claraline, leaving so soon? I do hope Henry performed to your satisfaction." She didn't take her eyes off mine.

"Oh yes," Henry said, deepening his voice to sound like Andre. "He was fantastic, as always. We ran into some old friends, though, and have decided to grab lunch. We work up such a hunger when we're here, as I'm sure you can imagine."

"Indeed. Hello Ava, Vivien. What an honor to see the Lilamoa sisters in my spa."

I stared back at her, haughty, imagining what Ava would have said. Viv beat me to it, practically purring, "Sshh. It needs to be our secret. Spiren likes us to keep chaste for our training, but I found my fire waning with no passion. A girl needs to be stoked every once in a while, wouldn't you agree?"

Annalee laughed, but her eyes remained suspicious. "Indeed. Perhaps next time you can call to let me know you are coming, I will arrange something special, befitting the Arch-mage's apprentices."

"That would be lovely," I said. Her eyes flashed to mine. Had she recognized my voice? Selene's hand tightened on my arm.

Annalee was motioning for one of the guards on the floor. We had to get out of here. Air began to swirl around my feet, my power rising.

Just then the front doors burst open and several men in uniform stepped into the room. In the distance, I could hear backup arriving, sirens from several directions.

Annalee's mouth tightened and I smiled innocently at her.

"It seems you have company. We'll leave you to your business," I said, inclining my head in a perfect imitation of Ava's proper manners. "The Circle thanks you for our most satisfying visit."

CHAPTER 25

masks of snow and ice
cool hot tempers, melt young hearts
like sweet summer treats

"Keep up the glamour for as long as you can, just in case she sends someone after us," I whispered to Vivien as we left the building.

Viv chuckled. "Okay, but I don't think we need to worry. She's gonna have her hands full."

Several cops zoomed by on motorcycles, air-driven sirens howling. Lyric and Jonah led the charge, with Lyric's attention fixated on the road. Jonah, always one to take in the scenery, went wide-eyed with recognition when he saw us, but he didn't slow. Hopefully he would tell his boss he'd seen us so the detective wouldn't worry.

The spa was in the same ritzy commercial district as the Enso, so we didn't have to go far. By the time we'd reached the Circle, Viv had allowed all of our glamours to drop. Henry and Selene gaped when I blew a puff of icy air towards the magically enhanced door and the steam-powered mech marched off its hinges to let us pass.

"Zow," Henry said. "How did you do that?"

"Magic," I said, and Viv winked at Selene.

"You mean, I could do that?" the slight girl whispered. Now that I could study her more closely, I wondered how old she actually was.

"Maybe not that, exactly. Everyone has different kinds of magic," Viv explained. "Some people can do almost anything, others, only a trick or two. But that's all you need to enter the Enso -- our doors will open at the even barest hint of magic."

"And without magic?" Henry asked.

"You knock, like everyone else," Viv said, but not without kindness.

"I can make myself invisible," Selene whispered.

Viv and I locked eyes, and I forced myself to smile down at the child. "Well, now. That's really something. Do you bend the light, so you're hard to see?"

"No," she said, considering. "Not like that. I just, wish no one could see me, and then, they can't. Like this."

Suddenly, she'd vanished.

Viv whistled. "Now that *is* something."

I heard a giggle by my side and I smiled as Selene reappeared. "That, my dear, is a rare talent. I think you've got real power in you."

She frowned. "They say my mom had real magic, too. But I don't think she did. Otherwise, why would she have worked at Blossoming?"

"Ah," Viv sighed. "Sometimes people wind up doing things they never thought they'd do. I'm sure she had her reasons. Now, how would you like to meet my sister, the real Ava?"

"Is she as nice as you?" Selene asked.

"Nicer," I said, laughing. Viv stuck her tongue out at me. "See?"

"I think I'd like to meet her."

"And I'd like to get back to my family," Henry said. "I need to figure out our next step, where we'll go."

"First things first," Viv said, sounding a bit like her sister. "This way."

Her voice had taken on a faraway quality, something I recognized as a tell-tale sign that she was communicating telepathically with Ava. She led us to the main library where we found Ava and the Arch-mage.

"You poor things, come, come." Ava was already halfway across the room, welcoming our refugees. "I have warm tea here, and cookies. Please, sit, sit."

"That's the Arch-mage?" Henry asked, awed.

"Yes, yes. Don't be frightened, he's just a person, like you or me," Ava reassured him.

"Only a lot older," Viv snickered.

Spiren only raised an eyebrow, remaining seated with a book in his lap. I knew he was taking pains not to scare them and I was grateful.

"And more powerful," Henry muttered.

"Don't worry, I only turn people into toads on feast days," Spiren teased. Selene giggled and I smiled down at her, handing her a plate of treats.

"You've been through a lot," Ava said slowly, sitting down next to Henry. "How much of it do you want to remember?"

"None of it. All of it? I don't know. I don't want to ever be so stupid again. The things I did, if my grandparents knew..." he trailed off, flushing with chlorophyll. "I wish I could forget any of it ever happened."

"I'm not sure that would be wise. But Viv and I, together, we have the power to gentle the memories, cleanse your energy fields and your minds so that while you might remember things, it will seem almost like it happened to someone else. The pain, the regret – those emotions won't be there anymore."

"You would do that, for me?"

"Of course we would," both cousins said as one.

"But I'm not a ket. I'm not one of you."

Viv frowned fiercely. "Not a ket, but surely a person just like anyone. What sort of people would we be if we didn't help you? Do you think the Enso exists only to protect our own people? This institution was put into place for everyone's benefit, to reassure kems, kets, and humans alike. Isn't that right, Arch-mage Spiren?"

Spiren looked up from where he'd been pretending to read. "Absolutely. So you do listen to me sometimes."

"Occasionally," she said with a smirk.

Selene giggled and I smoothed her hair, charmed. She looked up at me. "Can I have my energy cleansed, too?"

"Of course," I said. "But first we should probably try and find out if you have any family-"

"No!" she exclaimed, spitting like a wildcat, hair on end. "If I have family, where were they? They never came looking for my mother, or me. Can't I stay here? I want to learn magic, too."

"Um, I don't know." I looked at my cousins, who turned as one to the Arch-mage.

"We've never had a child at the Enso. How old are you, child?"

"My name's Selene," she said. "And I'm nine."

Younger than I'd thought. She was tall for her age.

"I know how to work. I could clean-"

"We have automatons for that," Spiren said, waving away the idea. Selene's face fell, and I felt the sudden urge to protect her, to leap at Spiren. Lucky for all of us, he continued. "It would be a good test of my apprentice's progress to see what they could teach you. Yes, I think I can make arrangements for you to stay." Selene squealed and ran to him, throwing her arms around his neck. The Arch-mage, usually so stoic, blushed and patted her on the head. "Okay. Don't cry. You'll have to go to school, too, and you won't work but you will have chores. It won't be all magic and starshine. Hush, there now."

Selene's sniffles had progressed to full-on sobs at the mention of school, and I realized she probably hadn't ever been allowed to attend or have friends her own age.

The cousins grinned at each other and my heart melted. "Looks like you're going to need to dust off those old babysitting skills of yours," I joked.

"What do you think I've been doing with you?" Viv sassed back and I wrinkled my nose at her. She winked, then turned back to Henry. "You ready?"

"Gods, yes. What should I do?"

"Just lean back and relax. We'll do all the heavy lifting," Viv assured him.

Henry slumped back in his chair and closed his eyes, his face beautifully serene. I stepped away, making room for Viv to sit at his other side. Each twin placed a hand on one of his cheeks, resting their other over his heart. They closed their eyes, and the work began. Spiren carefully moved Selene off his lap, motioning for her to finish her cookies, and came and stood behind me.

"You know," he said quietly in my ear. "There could be a place for you here, too."

"An apprenticeship?" I whispered, surprised.

I felt, rather than saw, him nod.

"Thank you," I said and meant it. "I'm honored. My heart belongs to the wilds, though. I'm not sure I could ever settle down to a life in the Circle."

"I understand. Your heart is what makes you such a good choice for a position here. If you ever change your mind, the offer will stand."

"I appreciate that, Spiren-san." I bowed deeply, stunned at the privilege he offered. "You honor me, truly. Perhaps some magic lessons, for now? Selene is not the only one who enjoys the prospect of learning."

The Arch-mage chuckled. "Indeed. I would be happy to teach you something whenever you're passing through. Please, consider the Enso your home in Chalinex."

CHAPTER 26

rabbits leap, home at last
flowers bloom, bright faces

Rabbit was almost over by the time I found myself returning back to the Enso to take the Arch-mage up his offer of a magic lesson. It had taken some time to help the Gunjabmi's out of the city, longer still to see them settled in their new home. The twins had sent word that The Blossoming was closed for good, Stinger behind bars for drug, sex and human trafficking violations. Relieved, I'd taken a week off to relax and get my bearings back, something I probably should have done long before. Now, I was back in the wilds, my pack heavy with mail, my boots pounding the hard earth up Mrs. Herold's lane.

Goats bleated, lambs trotted near the fence for a petting. Two men waved from a field where they were laying in new crops. Mrs. Herold's new helpers were working out fine, I noted happily. I scratched one of the lambs behind its ear and continued down the road with a light heart. When I climbed the steps this time, I didn't have to knock on any door. Mrs. Herold and Mrs. Gunjabmi were shelling peas on the porch, rocking their chairs slowly on either side of the table.

"Ohalo Omma, Mrs. Herold." I leaned down to kiss them each on their cheeks, the former's soft and flushed with a healthy tinge of sage, the latter's more worn and tan.

"I told you, call me Kass," Mrs. Herold tutted.

"Sorry, Kass, old habits die hard."

"Fern! Bee! Quit dawdling and bring the tea and onigiri!" Omma called.

A minute later two of Henry's sisters came out with a tray half their size laden with Kass's usual fare. Now, though, the rice balls weren't perfectly rounded and had clearly been shaped by smaller hands.

"You made these?" I asked them as they set down the tray carefully.

"I did," Fern answered, claiming her work with pride. "Those ones have roast lamb inside, and the ones rolled in sesame are sweet, filled with hazelnuts and cocoa."

"She's been making up some of her own recipes," Kass informed me, sounding pleased. "And going through my old cookbooks, making things I haven't had in years. She's got a knack in the kitchen."

Fern beamed. The girl had made a swift and full recovery within hours of Henry's return. He'd sat with her the whole time, while I'd talked through my plan with Omma and Pablo in the kitchen. Mrs. Herold needed help, I'd said, and she had a surplus of living space. I knew she'd welcome them with open arms, even the children. And if she didn't, or the family decided farm life wasn't for them, well, at least they'd be in a safe place while they figured out their next steps. Stinger would probably go away for a while, I'd explained, but that didn't mean they couldn't send people after Henry to punish him. It had been best, we decided, for the entire family to get out of the city as soon as possible. Agreed, we'd sorted clothes and keepsakes into bags while Henry sat with Fern and helped her heal in a way that only another Flora could. By midnight, we'd been on our way, laden with packs and sleeping bags, telling the children we were going on an adventure. We had spent the night in the wilds on the outskirts of the city, watching dragons shimmer and play in the fire as the children nodded off to sleep. It was their first time out of the Mudlands.

The girls ran off towards the barn, screeching when they got inside and then running back out, their brothers chasing them with sloshing buckets of water. Chickens scattered, flying in every direction and squawking at the disruption.

"They look happy," I said.

"They are," Omma agreed.

"Country air is the best thing for children," Kass said wisely, returning to her work shelling peas. "You did right bringing them to me."

"Yes, I'll never be able to thank you enough," Omma said. "This is so much better than Perseus ever could have been. Those old dreams seem a lifetime away, a fool's idea of happiness. Who would have thought such a beautiful life could be found here on Renga? The children glow now, they are so happy and free."

"Nonsense," Kass tutted, her voice thick. "Nikta didn't do nothing special. She just brought you home. Gave me a sister, brought home my family."

"I feel the same way." Omma reached over and held her new friend's hand. "I was telling Henry just the other day, everything he went through – he has to think of those times as holy, because they had to be fated. Didn't it all? Because it brought us all here, where we can be a real family."

"Aw. You guys, you're going to make me cry. Stop it," I said, gladness welling up inside me.

"It's true," Kass said matter-of-factly. "And you can't never stop the truth. I made them move out of those rickety farmhand quarters last week. Told them there weren't no sense in them staying out there when I had this big house to myself. I'm putting them on the deed, too." Omma's eyes went wide and she started to speak but Kass shushed her. "Don't you say nothing. I got a letter for Nikta just inside the door to deliver to my lawyer when she leaves, don't let me forget to give it to you," she told me. "I don't want that fool son of mine running anyone off my land should something happen to me. If he wants the farm, he'll have to come back here and share it. I don't see him coming back from his glamorous life up on that moon, and I'll be durned if he's going to sell it just to make some spending money. Not in my lifetime or after."

"Aw, Mrs. Herold, don't talk that way," I said. "I'm sure he wouldn't do that. He'll miss this place and come back someday."

"Naw, he won't. He loves the tech and the glitz up there on Hokku too much, I know it. But it's okay. I have young ones here enjoying the land and that's enough for me. And you're doing it again," she said, pointing a pea at me like a dagger. "I told you. Call me Kass."

"Yes, ma'am. I mean Kass."

"More tea?" Omma asked, already filling my cup.

"Yes, please." She overpoured and the sweet liquid dribbled over the rim of the glass, onto the table.

"Oh, dear! Let me clean that up for you. I'm so sorry," she said.

"No," I said, stopping her. "It's a blessing. My cup is overflowing," I reminded her of the Japanerican custom of over-pouring a guest's sake to invite abundance. "The gods smile on us."

"Aye, that they do," Kass agreed, toasting me and allowing her own cup to slosh a bit onto the table as well. Omma joined us and we all laughed, happy.

"You'll stay the night?" Omma asked, putting down her glass.

"Of course," I said, gazing out over the fields where Henry and Pablo worked as one, shirts off, bodies glistening with exertion. It was the best kind of sweat, the kind brought on from the honest labor of making your own way in life, a body's joy knowing it had become self-sustaining.

They'd found their place, their calling. And in helping them find it, in helping Selene, so had I. Today was a blessing, and tomorrow would bring a new adventure. I looked back at Omma, at Kass, and said the words of the fulfilled.

"There's nowhere I'd rather be."

GUIDE TO RENGA
An Appendix

Aligna's Well – One of Hot Creek's largest, deepest bathing pools. Dedicated to a Japanerican moon goddess of ancient Inuit origins. Long known in Prime as a wild holy place for ritual bathing and healing, now managed by the Night Seekers.

Allen – a PGPS Customs Master with stringent procedural standards.

Amaitomi River – Literally "Sweet Riches." Wrapping around the north and east quadrants of Chalinex, the gentle river was originally used to transport Chaline from local mines to processing centers. Its aquifers yield a sweet, mineral-heavy water that is believed to lend health benefits to the locals. On the far northeast side of its banks you will find the wealthiest citizens of Chalinex separated from the rest of the city by drawbridges.

Amarasu – A modern Japanerican amalgamation of Mother Mary and Amaterasu. A divine star-goddess, she is the patron of mothers, couples and fertility.

Arch-mage Juniper Spiren – head of the Chalinex Enso with a talent for swaying other peoples' emotions. Very tall and thin with long black hair and eyes that have laughed many times through his advanced years.

Ava Lilamoa – Twin daughter of Nikta Kozan's great-aunt, making her Nikta's first cousin. Ten years older than Nikta. Apprentice to the Arch-mage of Chalinex. Nearly identical to Vivien, white-haired and dark eyes like coal. Ava is long-haired, calm and cool.

Axel Lyell – Long-haired, low-level sleaze.

Baba – Informal word for obaasan, or grandmother.

Bakeneko – In folklore, a cat who has become a yokai spirit or demon, more of a benevolent trickster than the feared Nekomato of legend.

Bartholomew Hill – Old and blind ket wizard with a penchant for plants.

Bee Gunjabmi – Another of Henry's sisters.

Bex Montana – New Chalinex policewoman, working the front desk at Precinct 8.

The Blossoming Spa – A full-service establishment.

Bobby – PGPS trainee recruited by Nikta.

Boone – Master Sorter for the Carry-with-Care program in Chalinex City. Terse, not a smiler.

Bowen Lake – One of the largest fresh-water lakes on the planet, on the other side of the world from Prime.

Buddhism – Not a religion, but a philosophy of self-improvement, Buddhism honors no deities but aims the enlightenment of the self, the soul. Buddha is considered the first known human to raise himself out of suffering into nirvana, overcoming death and the underworld. After enlightenment, he made it his mission to likewise free humanity from the veil of illusion. Meditation, morality, detachment, and non-duality are encouraged.

Calressium – A silvery teal metal so rare and tightly controlled by the Peoples Galactic Confederation that almost no one else had access to it. Can only be cut by itself.

Carry with Care – The designation for any mail deemed too sensitive for electronic transmission or bulk transport, demanding the use of a Peoples Galactic Postal Service special carrier or post runner.

Cedar Secondary – The high school Nikta and Jonah attended. Wildcat Mascot.

Champagne – Club owned by Nestra Laroche.

Chaline – A clay-like substance that heals and nourishes the body.

Chalinex City – Big city to the east of Prime City. Dirty, corrupt, everything modern life has to offer.

Chalinex City Police Department – AKA, CCPD. Only the best and the brightest.

Chimeras – AKA, Kems. GMO-breeds of humans, including any blend of animal DNA with human. On Renga, most chimeras are descended from Japanerican miners who were engineered with panther-DNA for survival purposes. The kems of Renga tend to have magical powers, though some say something in the mines triggered other changes in their DNA to make them more in tune with the quantum field of Renga. Is it really just physics, masquerading as the unexplained?

Clive – Servant to Nestra Laroche.

Doc Brado – Family doctor in Prime City.

Elysienne Sonnet – Named after the Earth-poets of Elysielle, this typical fourteen lined, ten syllabled sonnet follows a haiku-inspired rhyming pattern of ABA CC DED FF GJG A. Themes generally juxtapose and center on emotions.

The Enso – AKA The Circle – A self-governing council for the magical kets of Renga. Ascribes to the ideals of harmony and balance, and that all are connected so there must be no harm. Its symbol is the medicine wheel, a circle made of the four elements (air, fire, water, earth) with spirit at the middle. Each local chapter is overseen by an Arch-mage.

The Feed – Dangerously addictive hallucinogenic drug. Untraceable, made with magic, prolonged use leads to apathy, starvation, and death.

Fern Gunjabmi – The eldest sibling after Henry, closest to him.

Florence Green – PGPS Sorting Master and Manager of the Carry with Care Program. Prior carrier, now in her sixties. Still keeps her nails filed razor-sharp.

Francine Sumisu – Jericha Sumisu's mother, retired schoolteacher, does piecework now to augment her pension. Husband ran off-world years ago. Empathic.

The Fringe – A planned community on Renga.

Galactic Credits – AKA credits, ceecees (plural) or cee (single). The e-money used throughout most of the GalCon. Two Galactic Credits are worth five Yendar, the local currency.

Galactic Frequency – The primary method of communication throughout the known universe.

The Gunjabmi Family – Omma and Pablo (aka Buelo). Their grandson Henry sends home money to help them care for his younger siblings. Live on Zenta Road, Block 14, Apt. 8JJ

Harai – Purification and blessing rituals held when the moon Sakura sets and the gods and ancestors leave Renga for a week-long period of holy rest.

Hari –Japanese acupuncture.

Henry Gunjabmi – AKA Rooster. Working a spaceship, saving up for a houseboat on Perseus for his grandparents and younger siblings.

Hokku – The smallest and closest of three moons. Just a dull blue rock, really, with a twenty-six-hour orbit. Where transports dock.

Hot Creek – Warmed by subterranean vents along its path, this long, sulphurous creek runs almost a hundred miles.

Innis McRory – Maeve Lewis's favorite nephew; son of Cadence McRory. Dark eyes, six feet tall, strong and gorgeous.

Japanerica – Tech-driven trading society from First Earth, a blended consortium of Japan, North America and Greenland that drove much of the original colonization and exploration of distant planets. One of the three major players in the United Galactic Front.

Jericha Sumisu - Blonde hair, small-earred ket. One of Nikta's old friends, now living in Chalinex City. Jericha works as a costume designer for the city's Opera house.

Jesse Tagazzi – Jericha's ex-boyfriend.

Jiji – informal term for ojisan, or grandfather.

Jimmy Lewis – Maeve and Maury's youngest son, errand boy for Otto.

Jin Black– The Berman's friend, a folk musician.

Joe – PGPS Customs Officer.

Joanie – Works Human Resources at the Chalinex PGPS. Tall and willowy, always happy to bicker with Vincent Sun.

Jonah Kozan – Nikta Kozan's twin. Once an Olympic hopeful, now a beat cop. Refuses to use his magic and passes for human. Has dropped his Settler's accent.

Joyce Finelli – Non-gmo human originally from Sector 89-T, dating Jonah Kozan. Works as a Sargent in his precinct. Short, fair, buxom. Her parents came to Renga as missionaries looking to save the world from false gods and magic.

The Kabuki – Dance club in Puraimura

Kami – The Enlightened Ones, Gods

Kami-mukae – Welcoming of the gods.

Kems – *See: Chimeras*

Ket – Feline-specific term for Kems on Renga. Most speak with a local accent incorporating slightly rolling r's, venturing into a trill when excited. They also tend to hum their m's. (*See: Chimeras*)

Kokuma Matsui – Jin's cousin from the White Rocks system, an off-world kem.

Kyogamura – Another early settlement on Renga, now a sizable city far to the south of Prime.

Lindsey – Jericha Sumisu's flatmate.

Lulu Wakanazu – Nikta's mother, died suddenly from a blood clot just before Nikta and Jonah graduated school.

Lunar Calendar – Adapted from Japanerican traditions, each month is named for one of thirteen zodiac signs: Thunderbird, Fox, Turtle, Cat, Rabbit, Dragon, Snake, Horse, Deer, Monkey, Owl, Wolf, Pig. The first day of each month there are festivals, offerings and parades to welcome the ancestors and deities back to Renga with the rising of Sakura.

Lyric Pearce - Lead Detective at Precinct 8 in Chalinex City. Warm honeyed skin and pale green eyes, wears a gold wedding band.

Matsuri –Festivals to welcome the gods and ancestors back to Renga when Sakura rises.

Maury & Maeve Lewis – Noodle Shop Owners, old friends of the Wakanazu-Kozan clan. Maeve loves peach wine.

Megain – Leader of the Night Seekers.

Mouse – A quiet bartender at The Ladybug.

Mrs. Kass Herold – Widowed Homesteader with a predilection for tea and talking.

The Mudlands – A deteriorating and dangerous neighborhood of Chalinex.

Nekokai – Derogatory term for the chimeras on Renga, loosely meaning "strange cat" or "faulty feline." Derives from the old demonic legends of the Yokai, Nekomato and Bakemato.

Nekomato – Monstrous cat demons (yokai) who hide in the mountains.

Nestra Laroche – AKA Lady Laroche. Second Daughter of Vice Consul Tindare of the Spartan Legions of Earth, widow of Lord Aganon Laroche. Entrepreneur with many admirers and suitors. Owns Champagne, a stripclub.

Night Potion – A potent, non-habit forming relaxation recipe passed down to Nikta from her mother using dreamless poppy (California poppy), kavakaa (kava kava), and lavender, blessed and extracted under the moonlight of Yuki for three cycles.

Night Seekers – A small religious group situated in the wilds between Prime and Chalinex, twenty co-op houses centered around the central temple hall.

Nikta Kozan – Ket mage descended from the Japanerican settlers of Renga. Post Runner/Special Courier. Fierce, independent and fast with the underscent of flowers. Follows her ancestral Shinto/Buddhist traditions.

North Bank – The wealthy section of Chalinex, divided from the rest of the city by the Amaitomi river in the northeast.

Novokyoto – Buddhist mountain outpost near the city of Kyogamura. Known for its potent pink sake.

Ohalo – Common Rengan greeting and farewell, generally conveying thanks, appreciation and blessings.

Onkoro Wakanazu – AKA Jiji or Ojisan. Nikta's maternal grandfather, the one who trained her for postal work

Otto Torriko – An unsavory character living in seclusion. Messy white hair, eyeglasses.

Oxby – Butler to Nestra Laroche.

Paisley Berman – PGPS Security Guard. Female, married to Sheila, no kids. Golden eyes, russet hair, curvy figure.

Peoples Galactic Confederation – AKA GalCon or the Confederation. The limited, liberal government protecting the rights of humanoid civilizations throughout the known galaxy. Individual planets retain authority over all matters except those delegated by the central government.

Pepe's Pedecurie – A one-stop shop in Puraimura for shoe repair and foot pampering.

PGPS – The Peoples Galactic Postal Service, and an arm of the Peoples Galactic Confederation. Primary delivery system for packages and sensitive communications on Renga.

Pheromones – kets can smell many things, including lies. When someone lies, they smell like sour milk and rotten oranges.

Post Runner – Special postal carriers employed by the PGPS for hand delivery of sensitive materials marked "Carry with Care."

Precinct 3 – Policing the Mudlands.

Precinct 8 – City police station where Jonah and Detective Pearce are headquartered.

Puraimura – AKA Prime City or Prime. The first city on Renga (its name actually means "prime settlement") where the initial mines and galactic offices were headquartered. Now hosts a large concentration of settler's descendants.

Qualitchka Vine – Rare floral source of a prized perfume made by only two perfumeries. The leaves and stalks have curative properties. It takes sixty years to mature; its purple and gold flowers bloom only once before the vine withers away and creates seeds. The seeds themselves are viable only for a short window of time.

Rae – Wolven teen kem from the Mudlands, manages Wild Things. Has a younger brother named Teddie.

Rama – Axel Lyell's young lover.

Regs – Said with a hard G, this is what kems call regular, non-GMO humans.

Renga - Nikta's planet. Despite its lack of a sunlit sky, the weather is mostly warm and humid owing to a sky filled with glowing nebulae and three moons. Originally settled and mined for its Chaline by Japanerican miners. The planet's own EMFs plays havoc with computer tech – making it difficult for modern tech to survive. Settlement and mining were difficult, but achieved. Shuttles must come and leave within hours, giving them just enough time to unload before their nav circuits are fried. Now, the planet attracts many people who are tech-phobic, such as health-nuts, criminals, religious zealots and homesteaders.

Reno Klein– Jericha Sumisu's flatmate. Gorgeous ladies' man.

Sakura – Renga's large pink moon (name means cherry blossom). With a twenty-six-day orbit, its passage marking the months and generally bringing several days of rainstorms.

Settler's accent – The kets on Renga hum their m's and slightly roll their r's, venturing into a trill when excited.

Shari – Mudland bully.

Sheila Berman – Professional chef. Female, married to Paisley, no kids. Dark skin, silvery hair, green eyes.

Shinko – Shinto processions to the temples in honor of the gods and ancestors.

Shinto – Ancient Japanese religion that melded with traditional Native American beliefs, incorporating the worship of ancestors and nature spirits with a faith in sacred power in both animate and inanimate things. On Renga, Shinto combines with magic and a strong connection to the elements of nature: terra, fire, water, air, and ether.

Spider – Magically animate automaton, greets guests and performs basic tasks for the Enso in Chalinex City.

Stephor Crane – PGPS Carry with Care Carrier, out on extended paternity leave. A reg.

Stinger – The elusive owner of The Blossoming Spa.

Tara – A feminine bodhisattva, or enlightened one, Tara is considered by Buddhists to be the mother of liberation. She guides humans towards loving-kindness, compassion and empty non-dualistic mind.

Time – Days on Renga are twenty-six hours long and based on Hokku's orbit, while years are based on Unified Galactic Time. Sakura orbits every twenty-six days, and Yuki has an irregular orbit that varies from two to three days. There are 13 months Rengan year, following the zodiac, and each week has thirteen days. Most people work two days on, one day off, with a two day weekend at the end.

Tom Kozan – Nikta's father. PGPS runner turned martial arts trainer, died in a bar brawl when she was fourteen. Preferred fists over magic.

Tulsi Flagg – Works at Nestra's club, Champagne.

Vincent Sun – Small, tough – head of the PGPS in Prime. Soft gray hair, cat ears, near black green eyes. Chunk out of one ear from a fight.

Vivien Lilamoa – Twin daughter of Nikta Kozan's great-aunt, making her Nikta's first cousin. Ten years older than Nikta. Apprentice to the Arch-mage of Chalinex. Nearly identical to Ava, white-haired and dark eyes like coal. Viv is fiery and dramatic with short, spiked hair.

The Wilds – the untamed, unsettled forests, plains and mountains of the southern hemisphere.

Wild Things – A club in the Mudlands.

Yendar and cents – the currency of Renga, used on the street though direct deposits are in galactic credits. Yendar is both singular and plural in form. Five Yendar are worth two Galactic Credits.

Yokai – Shapeshifting demons of Japanese mythology, some truly terrifying and evil, some mere tricksters, and still others, (mostly) benevolent spirits like the Coyote or trickster Fox of North American Indigenous legends. A common slur against chimeras on Renga.

Yuki – Renga's medium-sized moon, white and the furthest from Renga with an irregular orbit. (Yuki means snow, which Nikta has never seen.)

Zeddie – Gum-snapping elevator operator in a high-rent apartment building. A reg. Wants to be PGPS.

Zenta Road – One of the most dangerous streets in the Mudlands, mail there gets delivered under escort.

Zyzygy – Three-day semi-annual alignment event of Renga and its three moons. A time of feasting, dancing, and fertility rites.

About the Author

Ellis Logan lives a quiet life in New England, obsessing daily over superheroes and the gods of old. She spends her days corralling wild children, playing with lynx-eared kittens and talking to trees. When everyone is settled down and the owls begin to sing, you'll find her typing and munching on dark chocolate while faeries whisper stories in her ear.

Follow Ellis on Facebook, Twitter and Instagram
at **EllisLoganBooks**

Leave a Review Online and

Join Ellis's mailing list at EllisLogan.com

More Books by Ellis Logan

Shades of Valhalla
Fates of Midgard
Gifts of Elysielle
Heart Ward
Song Walker
Dream Tracker
The Warping
The Storming
The Burning
Post Magic

www.ingramcontent.com/pod-product-compliance
Lightning Source LLC
Chambersburg PA
CBHW032028240626
47154CB00003B/826